CREEPIN' WITH THE PLUG NEXT DOOR 3

BY:

NATIONAL BESTSELLING AUTHOR,

MZ. BIGGS

CREEPIN' WITH THE PLUG NEXT DOOR 3

Published by Cole Hart Signature, LLC.

Check Out These Other Great Books By Mz. Biggs:

See What Had Happened Was: A Contemporary Love Story (Part: 1-3)

Yearning For The Taste of A Bad Boy (Part: 1-3)

Dirty South: A Dope Boy Love Story (Part: 1)

Falling for A Dope Boy (Part: 1-3)

Feenin' For That Thug Lovin' (Part: 1-3)

A Bossed Up Valentine's (Anthology)

Jaxson and Giah: An Undeniable Love (Part: 1-2)

Finding My Rib: A Complicated Love Story (Part: 1)

In love With My Cuddy Buddy (Part: 1-2)-Collaboration

Your Husband's Cheating On Us (Part: 1-3)

From Cuddy Buddy To Wifey: Levi and Raven's Story (Standalone/Collaboration)

In Love With My Father's Boyfriend (Standalone)

Your Husband's Calling Me Wifey (Standalone)

She's Not Just A Snack... She's A Whole Buffet: BBWs Do It Better (Standalone)

Blood Over Loyalty: A Brother's Betrayal (Standalone)

Married to the Community D (Part: 1-2)

Creepin' With The Plug Next Door 3

Downgraded: From Wifey to Mistress (Part: 1-3)

A Mother's Prayer (Part: 1-2)

Heart of A Champion... Mind Of A Killer (Standalone)

Turned Out By My Husband's Best Man (Standalone)

Ain't No Lovin' Like Gulf Coast Lovin' On The 4th of July (A Novella)

This Is Why I Love You (A Novella)

The Hood Was My Claim To Fame (A Novella)

A Killer Valentine's (Anthology)

Bouncing Back After Zaddy Gave Me The Clap (Standalone)

Tantalizing Temptations in New Orleans (An Erotic Novella)

Santa Blessed Me With a Jacktown Boss (Novella)

Diamonds and Pearls (Standalone)

Dating A Female Goon (Standalone/Collaboration)

Pregnant By My Best Friend's Husband (Part: 1-2)

Wifed Up By A Down South Boss (Thug Love Collection)

Creepin' With The Plug Next Door (Part: 1-3)

Author's Note:

The feedback I've received from this series has been so amazing. I'm so glad I was able to provide you with something that would hold your attention and keep you wanting more. This by far has been one of my best series, if not the best series, that I've written. I really enjoyed the characters and bringing them to life. As always, I have to thank each and every one of you for the support you have given me. It does not go unnoticed at all. If it weren't for the support, I certainly wouldn't be able to continue doing something that I truly love. Thank you for rockin' with me. You didn't have to pick up my book, but you did and I'm grateful for that.

Now is the time that I ask for you to please take the time to leave an honest review on either Amazon or Goodreads after reading the book. Your support is greatly appreciated. Also, feel free to reach out to me anytime via the contact information listed below. Happy Reading... ☺

~Mz. Biggs

Want to connect with me? Here's how:

Email: authoress.mz.biggs@gmail.com

Twitter: @mz_biggz

Instagram: mz.biggs

Goodreads: Mz. Biggs

Facebook: https://www.facebook.com/authoress.biggs

Author Page: https://www.facebook.com/MzBiggs3/

Look for my Reading Group on Facebook: Lounging with Mz. Biggs

Where We Left Off:

Zelle

My baby had my babies. I was happy as fuck. Where we thought she was only having two babies, she ended up having three. That meant I was closer to getting my own football team. We had the space and the money, so why not have a house that would be loud with children running around and helping us make memories?

When I went to the nursery, I watched them run tests on the babies, and they had to put Baby C on oxygen because she wasn't breathing too good. That worried me, but the nurse told me that it was normal and not to worry too much. The babies were resting, so I left them in the nursery to go back to check on India. I told the nurse I wouldn't be gone too long, and I didn't want any shit when it came down to my babies. If I had to fuck up everybody in this damn hospital, I would.

It wasn't long before I was back in the room with India. She looked drained. Sia and her mother were saying their goodbyes. I was going to go ahead and take Mon back up to his room so he could get some rest too. He was mighty quiet through everything, but I'm sure I knew why. He was taking in everything that was happening so he would know what to expect when it was time for him and Sia to have their baby.

"You ready to go get in the bed?" I asked Mon.

"Yeah, I need to give you and sis some time together, and I'm sure she needs some rest."

"Aight. I'll take you back now." I turned and looked and India. "Baby, I'ma take him back up to his room, and I'll be right back."

"We can take him back." Sia stopped me.

"Naw. Zelle can take me back," Mon opposed.

"Well, I said that we were taking you back and I meant that. This ain't up for discussion. And I'm staying here with you until you are released so get ready to share that lil' bitty ass bed with me," Sia asserted. She was not playing with Mon. Mon smiled a bit. That let me know he was diggin' the fight Sia was putting up for him.

"Wait. Before everyone leaves, I think I know what I'm going to name them," India shouted. That caused everyone to stop what they were doing and focus their attention on her.

"What is it, baby?"

"Well... Baby A is the boy, and I can already tell he's going to be strong-willed and a protector like his father, so I'm going to name him Zellous Antonio Walker Jr. We can call him Z-2."

"I like the way that sounds, I told her. What about the girls?"

"Baby B will be Zella Antonia Walker. We can call her Z-3. And for Baby C, her name will be Zoelle Antoinette Walker."

"Let me guess, Z-4," I cut her off.

"Well, aren't you a smart little cookie," she joked.

"Whatever. I love the names baby." I pecked her on her lips and rubbed her forehead. There were beads of sweat forming. "You're tired, aren't you?"

"Yes, I'm very tired."

"That's why we're about to leave. Get some rest, and we'll check on you tomorrow," Sia told us.

Everybody hugged, and they were on their way out the door when the door flew open, and Link and Cynthia walked in.

"Where is everyone going? The party is just beginning," Link alleged.

"What the fuck are you doing here, and how did you get past security?" I barked.

"You know niggas will sell their mothers for the right amount of money," he answered. That was probably the one and only thing I'd ever agreed with his ass on.

I reached behind my back and was ready to shoot his ass where he stood. Mon had to stop and remind me that we were in the hospital. There was no where to hide the body and the noise from the gun would be too loud because I didn't have my silencer.

"We just came by to congratulate the lucky couple on bringing these wonderful babies in the world. We also have a push gift for my sister," Link announced.

He pulled his phone out and played with a few buttons before sticking it back in his pocket. All of a sudden, India's phone went off.

"We don't have to stick around for this part. Please know that we will meet again," Link shrugged, and he and Cynthia left the room.

"I'm going to follow them so I can kill his ass in the parking lot," I barked.

"Chill out, bruh. His time is coming." I was going back and forth with Mon about what I wanted to do. I never even noticed that India had gotten quiet.

"Sis, are you okay?" Sia asked. She went towards India to check on her.

India's phone dropped out of her hand and hit the floor. What I saw on her screen was what I knew to be the end of us. India wouldn't even look at me. There was no way I could explain the picture. I'd been caught red-handed. Never had I slipped like this, but this was surely one for the books.

My phone went off next, and I checked it. I already knew it was something that had to come from Link. When I opened the message, it was the same exact picture that was sent to India. Only my picture had the caption: **CHECK MATE!**

(To Be Continued...)

Chapter One:

Sianni

Today was one of those days where I wanted to click my heels together and be anywhere but here. India received a message that left her speechless. If you knew India, you'd know there was never a time when her ass didn't have shit to say. Right as she dropped her phone, Zelle's phone went off. He had no words, either. That caused me to move closer to India's bed to see what the hell had happened. The picture that was on her phone made me instantly mad. Not only was Zelle with another woman, but so was Mon. Those niggas were having a threesome in the middle of a damn club. *What kind of shit was they on? Somebody had to have slipped something in their drinks for them to be so damn careless. There was no way both Mon and Zelle could be that stupid.*

"I can explain," Zelle finally spoke.

"Explain what? There's nothing to explain," India replied. She struggled with getting out of the bed.

"India, baby, you just delivered, you need to stay in bed," Zelle reasoned with her.

Although I was upset, I agreed with him. "India, please sit back down. We can discuss this shit later," I cosigned with Zelle while giving him the side-eye. That nigga had the nerve to shrug his shoulders like he didn't know why she was angry.

Out of nowhere, India's phone went off again. This time, it was a video of Zelle and Mon with the same bitch from the picture. I can't lie, Link played the shit right. Anybody could photoshop a photo, but ain't no way they could lie their way out of a video.

"Do you not see this shit?" India asked me. "Our men are sitting there, fuckin' another bitch while they were with us."

"Technically, I was single, and I still am. Sia has no reason to be mad about some shit I did when we weren't fuckin' with each other," Mon spoke up.

"Mon, don't make me roll your ass down the stairs in that fuckin' wheelchair. Regardless of whether we were together or not, we were fuckin'. You fuckin' another bitch is fucked up," I fussed.

"Don't tell me about what's wrong when this nigga you fuckin' with showed me a video of you and him fuckin' on the damn balcony. You better count this shit as payback," he spat.

"You got me fucked up, Mon. I'm not one of these other thirsty bitches that you can cheat on, and we go on like everything is all good."

"Sia, shut the fuck up! We were not together, so how the hell could I have cheated on you?"

"Will you both please just shut the fuck up?" India roared. "Zelle, I'm going to ask you to leave. If I have to ask again, then I will call to have security escort you out," India very calmly spoke.

"I'm not going anywhere until we talk about this. Yeah, I fucked up, but it's not what you think. I was drugged." The way Zelle blinked his eyes let me know that his ass was lying. But I wasn't 'bout to get in the middle of their business unless India asked me to. I'd seen more than enough tv shows where a friend jumps in to help another friend, and it ends up backfiring on them. Well, that was not about to happen to me.

"Come on, Zelle." My mother had to stick her nose in their business. "I know you don't want to leave, but India just gave birth. She doesn't need all the stress. Yeah, she delivered the babies already, but she's still trying to recover. Anything can happen if she gets too upset."

"It's okay Mrs. Mitchell, I got this." India walked over to her bed and hit the button for the nurse.

"May I help you?" someone came over the intercom and asked.

"Yes, I have an unwanted visitor. I need security to come escort him out. Thank you," India quickly stated.

"We doing this now, India? You can't talk to a nigga that only fucked up once? I told you I was drugged. Look at the video. You can clearly see that I wasn't enjoying myself," he lied. That video showed him doing more than just enjoying himself. Zelle looked like he wanted to lay in that pussy all day. He had his head thrown back, and his fuckin' eyes closed.

"Wait..." India said. She picked her phone up and looked at something and put it back down. "You should've really died that night. Then, I wouldn't have had these babies by you, and I certainly wouldn't be here hurting." I knew then that India was really and truly hurt because she didn't remember that her ass was already pregnant before that night and because she made it seem as if she regretted having her babies. That was not in her character at all.

Taking the phone from India, I looked at the date and time stamp on the video to verify India's thinking. It was the same night that Mon and I had gotten into it and that Zelle was supposed to have been killed. After hearing what India just said to his ass, he probably wished he really had died.

"You don't mean that shit, India. You're just upset."

"Look at me, Zelle. I mean really look at me. I was a broken woman before I met you. I told you all the things I'd gone through. Shit that nobody else knows about me. Even things that I never told Sia and she's my best friend. But I trusted you. I broke down the brick wall I had up and let you in after you promised that you'd never hurt me. But you did. You're no different than the rest of these men out there in the streets. So, do me a favor and go join them. When the kids need something, I'll let you know. Until then, stay the fuck away from me." I can't recall the last time I'd seen India that upset. She didn't blink an eye or drop a tear. That was another sign that she was really hurt.

'Come on, Zelle," my mother told him again and ushered both him and Mon out the door.

If I never saw Mon again, I'd be okay with that. I'd finally gotten to a point where I was ready to walk away from Yosef and give my all to Mon and his ass out in the streets fuckin' another woman. If that would've been me with another man, he would've tried to kill my ass. Now, he was going to find out what really happened when you hurt me.

Chapter Two:

India

It wasn't until Mon and Zelle had left out of the room did I allow a tear to drop. He knew that he'd hurt me when I saw the video, but I wasn't about to let him see how much. Why give him that much power over my life?

"Are you okay?" Sia asked. I looked at her crazy for asking such a dumb ass question. Yeah, I knew she didn't mean any harm, but that was not the time to be stupid.

"How do you think I am? I done sat in here and allowed these babies to bust my pussy open and he out there cheating. Was he scared that my shit wasn't going to be tight and right after I gave birth? He just had to have somebody else lined up to please him, huh?"

"India, I don't think that was the case at all. He made a mistake."

"The same mistake Mon made?"

"Bitch, fuck Mon. He ain't shit!"

"If you're going to try to preach to me about my relationship, then I need to be preaching to you about yours. You really have no reason to be mad at Mon because y'all weren't together when this happened."

"That don't mean shit. He was trying to be with me. How he gonna tell me he a real man and that I needed to allow him to make me happy when he was out there hoeing around like Yosef?" Sia was mad, and I understood where she stood, but she was in the wrong when she slept with Yosef. She can't get mad at him for doing the same thing that she did. Plus, I don't know how many times she needed somebody to remind her that they weren't together when it happened.

"I hear you, Sia. I don't want to talk about this anymore. Can you give me some time to be alone?"

"I'm not sure you need to be alone right now," Sia alleged.

"Maybe I don't need to be alone, but I want to be. I'll be fine," I advised her.

"Okay, but you call me if you need me," she told me. I leaned down and gave her a hug before watching her exit the room.

The only people I could think to call were my mothers. They left after I'd delivered the babies because they wanted to give me time to rest.

"Hello," Momma Celia greeted me on the phone.

"Hey, ma. How are you?" I inquired.

"We're good. We can't wait to get back up there tomorrow and see our grandbabies," she told me. There was a brief moment of silence on the phone. That was because I was doing my best not to cry. But my best wasn't good enough. I started bawling my eyes out. "India, what's going on? Why are you crying? Tinnaaaa get your clothes on, we got to get to the hospital." Since I knew they were coming, I ended the call. I hated for people to see me cry, but these were tears that I just could not hold in any longer.

There I sat in the hospital bed, lonely and broken. Zelle was supposed to be my soulmate. The one I spent the rest of my life with. Yeah, I knew what he did to make money, and I knew that along with the money came bitches. But I trusted him enough to do the right thing when those hoes threw themselves at him. For me, pussy was the same no matter who you're inside of. However, that could just be me speaking from my perspective as a woman. But, if you aren't happy with the pussy you got, then leave it for someone else that'll give you what you need. Don't hurt the other person because you're only damaging them for the next person that comes along.

***

I'd dozed off to sleep. When I woke up, both of my mother's were in the room with me. Zelle was there too. For some reason, the babies had been rolled back in the room.

"What time is it?" I asked my mothers.

"It's two in the morning," Zelle answered.

"Mom?" I called out.

"Yes, baby?" Momma Tina answered.

"What time is it?" I asked again, rolling my eyes at Zelle.

"Baby, Zelle just told you it was two in the morning. What the hell is going on with you?"

"He's what's going on with me, and I'm not going to ask his ass again to leave," I muttered.

"India, if you want me to be away from you, then that's fine. But what you not finna do is keep me away from my kids. Now, I told your ass I fucked up, and I'm going to spend the rest of my life trying to make shit right with you because I want my family," he expressed.

"I don't give a damn what you said. I don't want shit to do with you. I'll call you when you can see the kids," I fussed.

"You a whole fuckin' lie. When your ass discharges, we are going back to the fuckin' house that we share so that my children will be in the same house as their mother and father. That house is big enough for you to be on one side and for me to be on another. My kids can go in the middle where we can each see them when we want to. Now, if you want to leave, that's your fuckin' business. But you not taking my kids anywhere and I'm not going anywhere."

"What the hell is going on with you?" Momma Celia asked.

"Zelle doesn't know how to keep his dick in his pants. He got mufuckas telling me his ass dead but he out fuckin' the next bitch. Go ahead and tell them," I ordered.

"That's not what happened. Mon and I were set up, and her ass can't even see that. Why the hell would I leave her to be with another bitch when I just found out she was pregnant? That was dumb as fuck. Why would I send my best friend to the appointments with you to keep me posted on what was going on if I wanted the next bitch?"

There was nothing I could say. The shit didn't add up, but I was hurt. I didn't want him near my children or me, but I knew that trying to keep him away from them would create even bigger problems between us and I didn't need that.

"Leave Zelle."

Zelle came over to my bed and pushed the button for the nurse. When she stepped in, he told her that he was stepping into the empty room next door and to bring him the kids once I'd fed them. The bitch had the nerve to tell him okay. But I was petty. Those babies would be getting fed until it was time for me to be discharged. He was not about to get shit his way when he was in the damn wrong.

Chapter Three:

Zelle

India had me fucked up. I stormed out of her room and headed to where Mon was. Visitation was over, but the nurses knew to let me past, or there was going to be a big ass problem.

"What the fuck am I going to do?" I asked Mon, who had sat up looking at me crazy.

"First, you're going to sit your ass down. All that walking in circles got me dizzy as fuck."

"I think I lost her. I don't know what I'm going to do without my rock, man."

"Again, sit yo mufuckin' ass down," Mon repeated. I was talking to myself so much that I didn't hear shit he was saying. He literally had to get out of his bed and touch me for me to sit the fuck down. The pain on his face spoke volumes, and I felt like shit for making him stand up.

"My bad man. I'm just so fucked up behind this shit. I can't lose her. That's wifey."

"Zelle, I told your ass not to go through with the shit in the first place. When you think you're going to get away with some shit, it always comes back to bite your ass," he preached.

"I know that. But damn. Why couldn't something else come up? This is destroying my baby."

"Give her some time to calm down and then try to talk to her. Don't force yourself into her life because that's only going to make things worse for you," he informed me.

"Yeah, but that's easier said than done. I can't imagine my life without her. And what if she takes my babies with her? Z-2, Z-3, and Z-4 ain't got shit to do with what goes on between India and me, but I feel like they are going to be punished for my fuck up." Mon started laughing. I stopped moving and looked at him. "What the fuck is so funny?"

"I know damn well y'all not really about to call those babies that bullshit," he queried.

"If that's what India wants, then that's what's going to happen." I paused. "I'm going to kill Link and Cynthia. They are her blood, but they've been hurting her more now that they're in her life than they did when they weren't. I bet Celia is the one that can track their asses down. She knows everybody in the fuckn' city, and she knows how to set some shit on fire without anybody knowing what really happened."

"Do you really plan on bringing her mother in on our bullshit? She could lose her job and her life. Don't do that shit."

"Well, tell me what to do. There has to be something to end this shit and get those two out of our lives."

"Let me think on it. Right now, I think it's best you go home and get some rest. Call India tomorrow and feel her out. If she answers the phone for you, then that means she's had some time to think. If she doesn't answer or if she answers and she's mad, then stay clear. The last thing you want to do is piss her off more."

Mon was talking with good sense. I could admit that it was going to be hard as hell for me to not talk to India. You don't understand how much of a struggle it was when I had to pretend to be dead. Every time Mon went to visit her, I made him take pictures of her and record some of the conversation so I could hear her voice. There were even times when I blocked my phone number and dialed her number so I could hear her voice when she answered. A few of those times she cussed me out for playing on her phone, and I'd laugh because of how feisty her ass was. That's really what drew me to her.

"What are you going to do about Sia?" I asked Mon.

"Not shit. Hell, we weren't together. Even when she was on that bullshit yesterday saying that we were together, that was her talking. I never confirmed nor denied anything. She can't get mad at me about something that happened when I wasn't with her."

"Yes, the fuck I can," Sia chided as she walked out of the bathroom.

"What the fuck?" Mon said. "How long have you been in there?" he asked.

"Long enough to hear you talking shit," she replied. Sia looked over at me and shook her head. "What the hell were you thinkin' Zelle? India loves you and deserves so much more than to be cheated on."

"I know that. It was never my intention to hurt her. Things just happened. Like I told her, we were set up. Right, Mon?" I looked at Mon, waiting for him to say something, but he never opened his mouth. "Really, nigga?"

"Mannnn... You not about to involve me in that bullshit. I don't know what happened other than Tiny tried to use her teeth to suck my dick and her pussy was so dry that I pushed her ass away."

"Yeah, but why did Pixie just bring her loose booty ass up there? She's never fucked with us or any other nigga before. Don't you get it?"

"Yeah, I get that much. But I also get that it was our choice whether to fuck her or not, and we did. We can't deny that. Plus, like I said. I don't owe Sia no explanation when I was getting my dick wet because she wasn't my woman. If anything, I should still be pissed at her for pickin' that chump over me and then fuckin' him on the balcony hoping that I would see. Yeah, he set your ass up. So, there is no reason for you to come in here trying to throw a fuckin' tantrum because I'm not dealing with that shit."

"Bu-"

"But my ass. You heard what I said, and I'm not discussing the shit again. I was single and had free range to do what I wanted." Mon put Sia in her place. She folded her arms over her chest, stomped her foot, and pouted.

Seems like she learned fairly quickly not to play with Mon's ass.

"I'm going to catch y'all later. I got shit to do," I told them. I dapped Mon up and gave Sia a hug. Whatever they were going through, I was sure could be worked out. All I could do was pray that India and I would be able to get shit back on track with us.

When I made it down to my car, I pulled my phone out. I hit Chucky up and told him to meet me at the spot. Mon was out of commission, but I sure in the fuck wasn't. I was on Operation Murk Them Bitches. Tiny, Link, and Cynthia had to die, and I wasn't going to rest until I saw that happen.

Chapter Four:

R'Mondo

"Why are you here, Sia?"

"I wanted to talk to you."

"Talk to me about what? If you think I'm about to be apologetic for fuckin' Tiny and Pixie, then you're wrong. You had a whole nigga so there ain't shit you can say to me. Besides, you cheated, not me." It was probably wrong for me to say that, but she needed to admit her truth.

Cheating to me was either sleeping with someone while you had a man or woman at home, becoming emotionally attached to someone while you have a man or woman, or being in a completely separate relationship from the one you already had and was still in. None of that shit applied to me. But it very well applied to her ass.

"Don't tell me what I did because we were both wrong. We both committed infidelity, and we fornicated, and in God's eyes, no sin is bigger than another."

"Don't come in here trying to act all holier than thou. You know just like I did that you wanted this dick and I gave it to you."

"Just like you wanted this pussy and I gave it to you."

"I never said I didn't want it. Shit, I'd been trying to make it mine for the longest, but you couldn't make up your damn mind on what you wanted to do. So, anything that happened after you went back to that clown ass nigga was on you, not me."

"So, you're blaming me for you sleeping with the next bitch?"

"Nope, but I'm blaming you for the fact that I was SINGLE when I did it. You're smart Sia. You know like I know that if we took this shit to court, then the fuckin' case would be thrown out. Be honest with yourself. You wanted a nigga, but you didn't want to leave the other nigga, and because of that, you pushed this dick to the next female."

Clearly, she didn't like what I said because she turned to go towards the door.

"I wish the fuck you would walk out that door while I'm talking to you. I'll fuck yo ass up, Sia." She stopped and turned back towards me. She had tears falling from her eyes. I rubbed my hand down my face because I couldn't believe she was going to cry over something she caused.

Was I wrong for talking to her the way that I was? Probably so, but why sugarcoat anything? If she was wrong, then she needed to admit it rather than try to make me feel bad about something I had every right to do.

"What the fuck are you crying for?"

"Because you don't see anything wrong in what you did."

"Sia, come here." She came right over to me. Only, she had her hands covering her face.

"Stop crying. You were wrong this time ma, and you're going to have to deal with the consequences. Had you made the right decision, then we wouldn't be here now. Like I told you earlier, I'm not going to apologize for something I wasn't wrong about. If you want to get mad at me, then that's fine. But what you aren't going to do is accuse me of cheating when I didn't. Cheating is not even in me."

"Then what do you call it?"

"I call it getting my dick ate and smothered. Fuck you thawt?" Okay, so I definitely shouldn't have said that, but I was just trying to make a point. She looked over at me, and I couldn't help but to stare into her beautiful eyes.

Sia had everything I could've ever dreamed of in a woman. She reminded me so much of my mother. I'd always told myself that if I ever decided to settle down, the woman would have to be someone that reminded me of my mother, and I meant that.

"Can we get past this?" Sia asked.

"Can you let that nigga you living with go?"

"Yes, I can. But you have to promise that you're not going to hurt me," she asserted.

"Sia, I'm a man, and I'm human. I'm nowhere near perfect. I fuck up at times, and I'm sure I'll fuck up if we decide to be together, but what you won't ever have to worry about is another bitch getting this dick that belongs to you. You know the kind of life I live, and you have to be willing to ride for me. That means long workdays, business trips, times I won't be able to answer my phone or return texts, other bitches getting in my face, and times when I don't come home. If you can't handle that, then we don't even need to talk about a relationship," I explained to her.

"I was with you until you said something about other bitches in your face."

"Out of everything I said, that was the only thing you paid attention to?"

"Anytime you mention other bitches, my mind seems to zone in on that and that alone because its those other bitches that land my ass behind bars," she stated and turned her nose up. I chuckled a bit because her ass was crazy as fuck. But I couldn't lie, that shit turned a nigga on. My damn dick was starting to grow under the damn sheet. I pointed at it so she could see what she'd done to a nigga and she started laughing.

"That shit ain't funny."

"Yes, it is, because you won't touch this pussy again until we discuss this other bitches thing," she quipped.

"Sianni, at the end of the day, there will never be a time where another bitch will be able to step to you about anything that I do. I'm a man of my word, and I can stand behind anything I do. So if I do something out of line, know that you'll hear about it from me before you hear it from anyone else. But I'm going to ask this one thing of you."

"What?"

"If a bitch does come to you on some bullshit, you talk it out with me and get my side of it before you start believing the shit because like I said, I'm a man that owns up to any and every damn thing that I do. Do you understand?" She nodded her head yes. That was all I needed to see.

"I guess you're happy to see me, huh?" she asked out of nowhere.

"That's random," I said before letting out a little chuckle.

"But that ain't," she replied, pointing at my dick sticking up and pressing the sheet up.

Licking my lips, I motioned for her to come lay down with me. Shidddd... I hit the damn button on my morphine pump to get something that would ease the pain so I could tolerate what Sia was about to do to me. She was wearing a dress which was perfect. She took her panties off and came to get in the bed with me.

"Siit on my lap," I suggested. Slowly, Sia straddled me.

"I don't think we should be doing this. I don't want you to get hurt," she told me.

"Girl, you better mount this bull." My dick was already at attention. It was only a matter of time before the medicine kicked in so I needed to bust a good one so I could lie back and relax with my girl. Damn, to call someone my girl was a lot for me, but it felt damn good saying it.

"I don't want to hurt you," she repeated.

"Fuckkkk..." I spoke through gritted teeth as she bumped the leg that I was shot in.

"Oh, my God! I'm so sorry," she cried. She attempted to move, but I pulled her down on my dick. One thing I could say about Sia was that her pussy was always wet and on go.

"Sssss..." she hissed. Still gripping her waist, I assisted her with grinding on my dick. Not even five minutes later, she took control and was riding the fuck out of me. The way she was bouncing had me ready to shoot some shit up. The morphine started to kick in, and I found myself becoming drowsy. "Damn, I missed this dick, Mon."

Sia started back grinding on my dick. She threw her head back and closed her eyes. For someone that had been shot, her ass sure as hell wasn't acting like it. I closed my eyes too. My medicine had kicked in, and I felt myself drifting to sleep.

Smack...

"Not until I get my nut," Sia stated, smacking me on my chest. My eyes popped open, and I looked at her ass crazy. "Sorry," she apologized.

Since the medicine shielded my pain, I started pumping up deep and fast. She started to moan loud as fuck. I grabbed the sheet and stuffed it into her mouth to shut her up.

Pfft...

She spit the shit back out. "I'm about to cum," she announced. That made me pump faster. She wasn't about to get her nut and I not get mine. A few pumps later, and I felt her juices dripping down my dick. It wasn't long after that I was shooting off inside of her. "Even when you're fucked up, you can still fuck," she joked. I couldn't do shit but laugh.

"Ain't nothing gonna stop me from pleasing my woman. I'll never leave room for another nigga to come in and do the shit that I'm supposed to do," I told her. She smiled and rolled over to the side of me. I turned as best I could to wrap my arm around her.

We laid in the bed holding each other until we both drifted off to sleep.

Chapter Five:
Sianni

(One Month Later...)

India moved back home with her parents to get away from Zelle. I never thought that she'd actually leave him because their relationship was always *#Goals* to me. Then the way she pulled it off was smart as hell.

Since Mon and I had made everything between us official, we'd spent more and more time together. So, what happened to Yosef? It's like his ass disappeared into thin air. When Mon was discharged from the hospital, he took me to the house I shared with Yosef. There was no sign of his ass anywhere. I even went as far as calling him to see if he would answer. Of course, he didn't. That led me to think he got the hint and moved on, but Mon told me not to be naïve. Yosef was lurking around somewhere and waiting on the right moment to reappear. That had me paranoid as hell.

Mon had some of his boys come and move all of my furniture out of the house. I found a home in the same subdivision where India and Zelle's house was. That was also where Mon lived before his house was destroyed.

He'd been staying with me while he waited on his new home to be built. That worked out perfectly fine for me because that only meant I'd have more time with him. The only time we were really apart was when we went to work or class.

"What took you so long?" India asked me when she opened the front door. Since India moved back in with her parents, Zelle had been on a rampage. He was furious about it, but it wasn't my business, so I stayed out of it. Every weekend, Mon and I would meet India and get the kids and then take them to Zelle. I wish they'd at least be able to co-parent for the kids, but it wasn't looking too good for Zelle.

"Sorry, I just got off work. What are you up to?"

"I have a date tonight."

"Say what now? India, tell me you're joking."

"No, I most certainly am not. Zelle threw our whole damn relationship away the moment he stuck his dick in that Pixie Stix bitch. It's time I live my life."

"Does Zelle know you're dating?"

"Nope, and you better not tell him either."

"No worries, my lips are sealed." Using my hand, I swiped across my lips and turned my hand like I was locking them. That made her laugh, which was something I hadn't seen her do too much of since she had the babies.

"What's up, sis?" Mon said, walking up out of nowhere. I'd rode to India's house by myself because he said he had some business to take care of and I was heading there straight after work. He came up behind me and wrapped his arm around my waist before placing his head in my neck. "You smell good," he remarked.

"Thanks, baby. What are you doing here?" I asked.

"We got done early, so I told Zelle I'd bring the kids to him," he replied. Then he looked over at India, "What's been up with you, sis?"

"Not shit. I'm going to get out a little tonight to enjoy myself. I'm long overdue for a night out," she told him.

"Word? Sia never told me y'all were going out," he commented.

"There was nothing for her to tell because she's not going with me," she stated. Mon paused briefly and looked at her. One of his eyebrows raised up, so I knew there was about to be some shit.

"Where the fuck you going, India?"

"That's for me to know and you to find out."

Mon took his phone out and made a call. He put the phone on speaker and smirked.

"Sup?" Zelle answered the phone. India's facial expression changed. She looked like her ass had just seen a damn ghost.

"You and India back together?" Mon asked.

"Naw. She still trippin' on that Pixie shit. I'ma kill Link for sending her that bullshit and that bitch Cynthia too. They just had to mess up our moment," Zelle fumed.

India was about to say something, but I stopped her. Mon could be petty at times, and this was one of those times. If she opened her mouth to say something, that would've been grounds for Zelle to question her ass. "Why you ask me that? Did she say something about it when you went to get the kids?"

"Naw. She ain't say nothing like that."

"Oh, damn. What she talking about then?" Mon began to laugh. India had a pleading look on her face as if she were begging him to keep his mouth shut, but Mon wouldn't listen.

"She said she's going out tonight. But get this shit... Sia ain't going with her," Mon confessed. I wanted to kick his ass in the shin for being so damn messy.

"Hand her the phone," Zelle roared.

"He don't have to hand me shit. I can hear your ass loud and clear," India spoke up.

"Where the fuck yo lil' ass going?"

"To mind the business that pays me; something your ass needs to be doing," she refuted.

"Don't make me f-"

"Fuck me up," she cut him off. "You done said that a thousand times and ain't done it yet, so get the fuck on. I have shit to do that don't involve you. Now, get the kids and enjoy your night," she spat and turned and walked back in the house.

"Where the fuck is she going, Sia?" Zelle questioned me.

"I honestly have no idea, and if I did know, I wouldn't tell you because she's my girl. Mon was wrong for even getting his ass on the phone and calling you," I fumed.

Glancing over at Mon, I rolled my eyes. His ass was going to hear my mouth behind that shit because he was wrong. While he was so busy trying to tell on India, he should've been telling Zelle's ass to keep dick to himself.

"Aye, I gotta go. Sia not bout to put my ass on punishment. I need the pussy like I need air to breathe." That shit made me laugh because he was so damn silly at times.

"Y'all take the babies to your crib, and I'll swing by to get them later," Zelle requested. That was fine by me because that gave me the chance to spend a little more time with them. Since India and Zelle had been going through their little situation, I haven't been able to spend as much time with them as I'd like to. So, any chance that I got with the babies, I took it.

Mon ended the call and told me he'd take the babies on to the house. He asked me to stop and grab us something to eat, and he'd pick a movie out for us. He wanted to have a date night which was cool with me. But I wanted to know how he really expected that shit to go with three babies in our presence.

Chapter Six:

India

Mon made my damn ass itch. He didn't have any business getting on the phone and telling Zelle what I had going on. I understood that he and Sia wanted us to get back together, but I didn't see that happening. For some reason, I just couldn't forgive him for cheating on me. That shit hurt worse than a damn bullet if you asked me. This love shit cuts deep as fuck and I didn't think I wanted to experience it ever again.

Standing in the blinds, I watched as Mon loaded the babies inside his truck. Sia went in a completely different direction as him. I figured he was going to meet Zelle by himself, which was okay. Plus, I needed to talk to Sia anyways.

Running to my room, I picked my phone up and dialed her number. I had to call three times before her black ass answered.

"Hello," she sang through the phone. Mon was truly making her happy, and I loved that because she had a good heart and deserved nothing but the best if you asked me.

"Hello hell? Why the fuck you didn't answer the phone?"

"Sorry, I was on the phone with Mon."

"Didn't you just see his ass?"

"Yeah, but you know how new love is."

"Whatever. What are you getting into tonight?"

"Nothing. Zelle is coming to pick the babies up from our house later," she expressed.

"Our house?" I asked. That was just me being funny.

"You might as well say it's our because he's been here since he got out of the hospital," she explained.

"Sia? You are so damn crazy," I told her.

"What do you mean? What I miss?" she responded.

"Do you notice that they haven't even tried to fix Mon's house? That nigga not trying to get that house fixed or buy another one because he's trying to stay up under your ass," I explained. She got quiet for a minute.

"Well, I enjoy his company. It's so much better than Yo-Yo's aggravating ass," she commented. I couldn't help but laugh because Yo-Yo did get on everybody's damn nerves. "When are you going back home?"

"I'm not. And you better not say shit to Mon or Zelle about my date. If you do then I'm not fuckin' with you anymore," I threatened her. It was no point in threatening her because I knew she was going to keep her mouth shut. But I felt the need to do it anyways.

"Bye, bitch! The only pussy I'm worried about is mine. Go on your little date. Maybe it'll help you see that Zelle is the man you need to be with. I gotta go though. Bye!" She ended the call without giving me a chance to say goodbye back.

My parents weren't home which was good for me because I could get dressed without them asking me a trillion questions about where I was going and who I was going with. They went out of town for the weekend, which they often did because they said it was the way that they rekindled their love and doing things together keeps their relationship on track. At one point, I believed that. But when I attempted to do that shit with my relationship, it backfired on me.

Inside my junky room, I dug through the different piles of clothes looking for something to wear for tonight. I settled on an all-black bodycon dress that hugged every one of my curves. The only thing I hated was the little baby pouch I still had from delivering the babies. I'd learned to embrace it, but you'd better know a bitch was working overtime in the gym to get rid of it.

Once I was dressed, I called my date to see if he was ready. I was going to meet him at the restaurant because it was too soon for me to be telling anyone where I lived. Reason being? I met him online. That speaks for itself.

My mind pondered on if I was doing the right thing. I loved the hell out of Zelle, but it was hard for me to ignore the fact that he cheated. Plus, I felt like I'd be a hypocrite to stay with him after fussing at Sia for always staying with Yosef when his ass cheated on her. I was so consumed by my thoughts that I was pulling up at the restaurant before I knew it. We were eating at Red Lobster because that was my favorite restaurant. I also thought that it was too soon for him to really be splurging on me at a fancy restaurant anyway. Being that it was imperative for me to fill him out first, this would be the perfect place for me.

Me: If I text you 9-1-1, you know what to do bitch!

I sent Sia a text to be on standby in case I needed her.

Bestie Bitch: Lmaoooo... We haven't done that shit since college. Give me details.

Scanning the parking lot, I checked to see if I was able to see my date getting out of the car. Nobody looked like the man I'd met online. I arrived a few minutes early just so I could try to get his license plates to send to Sia. But since I didn't spot him, I sent Sia a picture of him.

Bestie Bitch: Damnnnnnn... He fine FINE. He got a brother?

Me: Get off my line. You not about to have Mon trying to fuck me up.

Bestie Bitch: Aye, it never hurt anybody to have a backup plan.

Sia's ass was retarded. She was talking major shit but let her see Mon texting some shit like that to Zelle, her ass would stroke the fuck out.

Me: His name is Clifford.

Bestie Bitch: Lemme find out your ass on a date with the big red dog...lol

That bitch had me in tears laughing at her ass. That girl got on my damn nerves at times, but I swear I couldn't imagine my life without her.

"Hello beautiful," a deep baritone voice said from behind me.

"Clifford?" I asked. Slowly, I turned to face him. I was shocked. He was not the man that I'd seen on all the pictures online.

"In the flesh," he replied.

The man standing before me had to be a joke. He was maybe five feet even and looked like a black Santa Claus. His belly hung over his waistline, his head was bald, and he had a long grey beard that touched his chest. Please don't get me started on his teeth. His teeth were yellow as hell, and his breath smelled like cat shit.

"I'm sorry, I think you may have me confused," I told him.

"Naw. You're the woman that I've been chatting with over the past few weeks."

"You Catfished me?" I asked. I was highly pissed off. He started talking to me, and I whipped my phone out like he wasn't saying shit to me.

"I was letting you get to know me. Most people only care about looks. That's why I made it a point to talk to you for a while so you could get to know me. Are you telling me that you no longer want to deal with me?" He raised a brow. What he said made sense, but it wasn't moving me.

"Look, I understand what you're saying, but that shit don't mean anything to me. What matters is that you lied!"

"Are you telling me that you would've still talked to me if I would've sent you a picture of what I really looked like?"

"I don't know, and I guess we'll never know because you never gave me the opportunity to decide if I would or wouldn't. You don't make decisions for people. Shit, you talking about getting to know you and that's cool. But I don't want to waste my time getting to know somebody that I can't look at and want to fuck. And trust me when I say you are not that person," I fussed.

Clap... Clap... Clap...

"I came down here to drag your ass back to the crib, but I think I'ma let you stay here." Zelle came out of nowhere and was clapping.

"How did you know where I was?" I asked.

"I always know where you are. Don't worry about how I know, just know that I know."

"Excuse me, but we are in the middle of a date," Clifford told Zelle and grabbed ahold of my arm. While I wanted to snatch away from him, I didn't. I glanced back at Zelle and rolled my neck.

"Aye bruh, this ain't what you want. You better take your Land of the Gnomes looking ass on with that bullshit," Zelle roared. I was about to say something, but Clifford stopped me.

"I got this, baby. This must be that old chump that you said didn't appreciate what he had," Clifford stated. I dropped my head. When I spoke to Clifford about Zelle, I never thought the shit would backfire on me, or that Clifford would bring the shit up to Zelle. Hell, I never expected them to meet. Luckily, the only thing I told him was that I didn't feel appreciated by Zelle.

"What you say to me, nigga?" Zelle barked. His tone got deeper, and his fists were balled.

Right then and there, I wanted to drop to my knees and pray my way out of this situation. The way Zelle was looking had me thinking there was no way I was going to make it out alive. Y'all pray for ya girl.

Chapter Seven:

Zelle

India had me fucked up. When she said she was going out and Sia wasn't going with her, I already knew she was going to be on some good bullshit. I asked Mon and Sia to take the triplets home with them, and I would grab them later. That would give me enough time to roll up on India and dead whatever shit she was trying to keep a secret.

Apparently, India forgot the amount of pull I had. All I had to do was make one call and have someone trail her ass any and everywhere that she went. Luckily for me, I still had access to her iCloud information and could track her phone. The minute I rolled up on her, I was killing myself laughing. She was ready to stop fuckin' with me just so she could get down with an Ommpa Loompa. Then she had the nerve to talk to him about some shit that was going on in our relationship. That shit hurt a nigga bad, but I wasn't going to let her know that.

"I don't know you, and clearly you don't know me, or you wouldn't be talking that slick shit. Don't fuck around and take your last breath in this damn parking lot," I barked.

The nigga had balls the size of a grapefruit because he walked up on me. India's face turned pale. She knew dude was making the wrong move.

"Clifford, I wouldn't do that if I were you," India warned him.

"Naw, let him do it. He wants to see me act a damn fool out here."

"No, he doesn't. He's sorry," India apologized for him.

"Don't speak for me, woman. I can speak for myself. He thinks because he's taller than me that he can say what he wants. He may have done that shit to you, but he sure as hell won't be doing it to me."

"What the fuck is that supposed to mean?" India turned to confront him.

"It means sit your ass down somewhere and let me handle this shit like a fuckin' man," he grunted.

Bowwww... Crackkkk...

That was the sound of me punching him in the jaw and something cracking. Blood spilled out of his mouth.

"Muthafucka," he cried and came running towards me. He was wildly swinging with his eyes closed. When he got on me, I grabbed the back of his head and rammed it into the back window of India's car. The glass instantly shattered.

"What the fuck, Zelle?" India yelled. But I had long drowned her ass out. I went to work delivering blow after blow to the nigga before dropping his ass on the ground.

Chucky jogged towards me and pulled me back. That was the only reason I stopped hitting his ass.

"You're paying for this shit, Zelle," India shouted.

"Fuck you, India. I fucked up. I told you what happened that night, wasn't me. I was drugged or something because I'd never stick my dick in another bitch, knowing that I had a woman at home that was my ride or die. You're so stuck on wanting to punish me that your dumb ass ain't trying to hear a nigga out," I spat.

Many people thought that I cheated on India for no reason. That's not the case at all. Something was off that night. Something had to have been put in our drinks because neither Mon nor myself were acting like ourselves. I mean come on, what nigga you know still wanna fuck after a bitch had done bit his dick?

"The fact that it has only been a month, and you're already trying to move on says a lot. But don't worry, I'm not about to chase you or stand in the way of your happiness. Just know that when you see me with the next bitch, you don't need to open your fuckin' mouth because this was a decision you made for the both of us."

"What the fuck you mean about the next bitch?" She got up in my face like her lil' ass was supposed to scare me or something.

"Exactly what the fuck I said."

"You not about to have no trout mouth bitches around my babies."

"They are half yours and half mine. What I do with my half is my fuckin' business. Now get the fuck out of my way before I move your ass," I cautioned her.

There was nothing left for me to say, so I went on about my business. Chucky drove me to the restaurant because I had high hopes that India and I would make up, and we'd ride back to our house together. Of course, that didn't turn out the way that I'd hoped.

As soon as we got inside of Chucky's vehicle, I hit Mon up to let him know what had happened and that I was headed to pick the babies up. Then, I went ahead and blocked India's ass from my phone, and from all of my social media accounts. I even went as far as blocking her ass from my email. She wanted to play hard, so I was going to show her that I wasn't the one to be playing with.

On the way back to the crib, I had Chucky stop me by Popeye's to get a couple of those chicken sandwiches.

"You good, bruh?" he asked while we were sitting in the drive-thru.

"Yeah. Never been better," I lied. I was feeling some type of way about the way India was acting. How the fuck was she so ready to move on after one month of us being separated? Not one time had she tried to talk to me and find out what happened that night. I understand she was hurt and she had every right to be, but why just throw our whole relationship away without finding out the truth?

"You don't have to lie to me. I know what it's like to be hurt. That's the main reason I don't date now. I fuck 'em and leave 'em," Chucky explained.

"That's what I'm going to do from here on out. I'd call for some pussy now, but India's so heavily on my mind that pussy is the furthest thing from it right now."

"I feel ya. But you know I'm here for you if you ever need to talk."

"Thanks, man. You're one of the realist niggas I know. Keep that shit up, and when we do this takeover, you already know there's a big promotion in your future." We dapped each other up.

With the food in the car, we headed straight for Mon and Sia's house. India's silly ass was there when we arrived, so I sent Chucky in to get the kids. India came out to the car trying to talk to me, but I picked my phone up and acted like I was on an important call.

Chucky and Mon put the kids in the car while India stood at my window. I wouldn't let it down for shit. I told Mon bye when he snapped the babies in.

"Shut the door," I told him. As soon as he shut it, I saw India step towards it. I hit the lock so fast on her ass, she couldn't say shit. She stumped her damn feet like a two-year-old. I leaned over and unlocked the door for Chucky. When he was in, I had him take me on to my house.

It was lonely in the house without India, but I made it a point to keep myself busy. If the triplets weren't with me, then it was Mon, Chucky, or one of the other crew members. We stayed on the go devising a plan to get rid of Cynthia and Link. One thing I noticed through this all was that Mon's Uncle Rocko was taking us to a bunch of bullshit ass meetings, but never really running the game to the streets down to us. We knew a lot as is, but there was some shit that we needed to know from him that would help us be even more successful as top dogs. Niggas feared us, but we wanted them to fear us on the same level that they feared Uncle Rocko. I'm not sure what it was, but he was moving funny to me, and that was something that was going to have to be discussed with Mon.

Chucky helped me get the babies in. I had him take them up to their room while I got their bottles together. Joining them in the room, I had Chucky start feeding Zella while I bathe Zellous. Zoelle's lil' ass was sitting there looking me upside my head. It looked like she wanted me to hurry my ass up, but she was just going to have to wait. By the time I was done with Zellous, Zella was still eating. She was just like India. She moved at the beat of her own damn drum. I laid Zellous down and picked Zoelle up to bathe her. She loved when the water hit her body. We could tell by the big smile that always appeared on her face.

Chucky had burped Zella and was now feeding Zellous. I went ahead and gave Zella her bath and laid her down to sleep before I started feeding Zoelle. Chucky had finished feeding Zellous and burped him. After he laid him down, I told him he could go ahead and leave. I used my phone to lock the door and set the alarm.

With all the babies in their cribs, I sat and waited for them to fall asleep before I headed to my room. A nigga was tired as fuck. The shit with India only added on to the way I was feeling. So much had gone on these past few months that I felt like I needed a "do-over." That shit with Pixie would be the first thing I did over. She wouldn't even get the chance to be in my presence.

It took me giving myself a little peptalk before I forced myself to get up and go to my room. "What are you doing here?" I asked India when I saw her ass naked in our bed with her legs spread open. She was playing with her pussy, doing her best to entice me.

"I'm ready to come home. I'm sorry about earlier."

"You ready to come home or you just ready for this dick?"

"Both. We can talk about me coming home later. I'm ready for that dick, now," she commented. I shook my head at her. That was all I could do. Normally, I would've told her no because of the way she'd been acting and because her ass was still recovering from birthing the triplets, but it had been a month since I got my dick wet and it was long overdue.

Wasting no more time, I slid out of my clothes and slithered on in the bed with her. I didn't try to engage in any foreplay or anything. My dick was rock hard from the moment I saw her playing with her pussy, so I slid right into her with ease.

"Sssss..." she hissed. "Hold on, baby. I gotta readjust," she exclaimed.

Instead of pulling out of her, I laid there for a good three minutes before I started gliding in and out of her. Her pussy was so fuckin' wet. It took everything in me not to bust so fast.

"Let me ride it, baby," she requested. I didn't move. In fact, I didn't say shit. The whole time I was fuckin' her, I was moaning in my head. She was not about to see how much I was enjoying being inside of her. She tried to kiss me and each time she tried, I turned my face away from her. "Kiss me."

"Naw. I'm good," I replied and sped up my stroke speed. For some reason, my mood was lost. The thought of seeing her with that Clifford dude came across my mind, and I pulled out of her. "You need to leave," I demanded.

"What? Why would you want me to leave? For the last month, you'd been begging me to come home so we can talk about things."

"Yeah, and each time I asked, you never came. The only reason you're here now is because you know you fucked up just like I did when you went on that date. Ain't no coming back from that shit, India. All I care to do with you at this point is co-parent. Now, leave," I asserted.

"You can't be serious. You're mad because I went on a date?"

"No, I'm mad because after what's about to be three years of us being together, you were so quick to give up on us. You know like I know that it don't take shit for me to get pussy from anybody, but I didn't touch a soul because I was waiting on you. That said a lot about my character. The fact that you meeting niggas, God knows where, and going out with them shows that we didn't mean shit to you. Now, I'm asking you to leave." She stood before me with tears raining down her face, but that didn't move me. I picked her clothes up and handed them to her. Pulling out my phone, I unlocked the door and turned the alarm off. "You can see your way out," I told her before I picked up my clothes and headed to the bathroom.

"So, you're just going to throw our whole relationship away?" she yelled behind me. I paused and turned towards her.

"India, I'm not even about to address that stupid shit with you. You know damn well that as soon as you saw those pictures, you tossed my ass to the wolves. Now because I found out about the little date you called yourself going on, you're worried about our relationship. Bye Felicia!"

"Fuck you, Zelle!"

"You just tried, and that didn't work out for you. I'll pass on that from here on out," I told her. I was only doing that because I wanted to get under her skin. I wanted her to hurt the way that I had been hurt.

Chapter Eight:

India

"You are not about to do this to me. You are the one who cheated on me with some prostitute," I yelled at Zelle. I was angry at the way he was acting. He'd beat the hell out of Clifford whom I was sure would call the police on him

"India, gon' back to your parents' house where you were staying. We can talk about this shit some other time," he refuted.

"Some other time like when?"

"Some other time like when I feel like fuckin' talking about it. Now, gon' head on with that bullshit," he grunted and walked on in the bathroom. He slammed the door behind him.

Instead of leaving like he told me to, I took it upon myself to go to the other side of the house like he'd suggested earlier. There was no reason why we couldn't co-exist in the same household, right? I'm sure if he knew that I was still there, he'd be upset, but I didn't care. This had to be fixed. We needed to talk about what happened. It was all too much for me earlier, so I wasn't ready to listen to him. Now, I was.

Swinging the door open to the first guest room I came to, I walked straight to the bed and flopped down on it. It didn't dawn on me to shut the door because Zelle hardly ever came to this side of the house. So, there was no reason for me to believe he'd come this way tonight. I was so wrong because I wasn't in there a good ten minutes before his ass came in there hollering.

"Get out, India!" he roared. I could've sworn I felt the house shake because of all the bass in his voice. He came marching inside the room that I was in.

"How'd you know I was still here?" I asked.

"Because of the fact that the alarm didn't beep alerting me that one of the doors had been opened. Now, get the fuck out."

The way Zelle had the house set up, whenever the alarm was on or off, it would still alert you if there was movement in the house or if one of the doors or windows had been opened. That shit got on my nerves because whenever I wanted to sneak up on his ass, I couldn't.

"Don't talk to me like that. My name is on this house too," I cried.

"I don't give a damn. You wasn't saying all that shit when you decided to go to your parents' house last month. I can't deal with you being here right now."

"No, what you want to say is that you can't stand to look at me."

"That's not what I said."

"You don't have to say it. Ever since I've been in this house, you have yet to look me in the face. Why? Are you disgusted by me? I didn't have sex with anyone else. I've been faithful to you since day one. So, you don't get to look at me in disgust."

"If you think I'm disgusted by you then you obviously don't know me at all. I'm disappointed in you more than anything. You wanted to break up, and I gave you what you wanted. If you want to go date, then so be it. What you do with your pussy and who you do it with is your business." He had started to piss me off more than he hurt me. That wasn't a good thing. He should've known that from hurting me in the past.

"Now, it's my pussy? What happened to it being your pussy?" I questioned.

"What the fuck are you asking me that for when you were out with that dorky lookin' nigga, ready to give it to him," he grunted.

"Just because I went on a date with him doesn't mean shit. I'm not a hoe, Zelle."

"You fucked me on the first date. Who's to say that you wouldn't fuck him too?"

"Fuck you, Zelle! You cheated on me. You don't get to talk to me like that!" I snapped. I ran up on him and started pounding on his chest. He just stood there as I tired myself out.

"You done yet?" he asked. I nodded my head. "Good," he told me and walked away. I chased behind him. He stepped inside the room. Standing there, my eyes followed his every move. He started throwing clothes in a bag. Still, my eyes watched him wondering where he was going to go. He turned to face me and handed me the bag. "Have a good night," he said and ushered me towards the door.

"What are you doing?"

"Helping you leave since you apparently can't find the door." That stung the hell out of my heart. Not my heart, my soul.

Zelle had never been that cold to me. How the hell did a situation that started off being about him end up being about me? It didn't make any sense. There was no reason for me to continue to put up a fight because he was stubborn as a mule. The only thing I could do was give him space. Dropping my head, I left the house that we'd created together. Even though it was not something I wanted to do, it had to be done.

When I got outside, it felt like I was making a mistake. Giving him space would've been the right thing for me to do, but then I thought about what I'd done. When I asked him for space, and he gave it to me, my mind wandered, and I started looking for someone else to date. What if he did the same thing? There was no way I was going to give another woman a chance to come in and take my place. Zelle and I had overcome too much bullshit to get our relationship to what it was before all this mess started. I was not about to walk away from him. Not now. We had a family to think about.

Storming back inside the house, I went right back in the bedroom. Zelle was just about to step in the shower when he saw me.

"What are you doing? I know I told you to leave."

"Yeah, you did. But as long as my name is on this deed and we have kids together, I will remain in this house." He didn't respond. He just stood there staring at me. Those few minutes that we were in an intense stare off seemed like forever. When the silence was broken, it was Zelle who'd broken it.

"You stay here. I'll be back," Zelle finally told me. I tried to stop him, but he wouldn't listen. He threw some clothes on and left the house.

The only place he'd be going so late was to Mon and Sia's house, so I wasn't worried. He could stay the night there if he wanted, but if his ass thought he wasn't ever coming home, he was sadly mistaken. I was dragging his ass back to this house tomorrow; no matter what.

Chapter Nine:

R'Mondo

"How are you feeling?" Sia asked me.

"I'm okay. Just a little sore. You good?" I replied. It had been well over a month since I'd gotten shot, but I still found myself feeling pain in my leg. That shit had me thinking I had arthritis or something.

"Let me put some of this on you," Sia insisted. She stood up and grabbed the Biofreeze off the nightstand. She kept it nearby because the pain in my leg was constant.

The whole time Sia moved, my eyes were trained on her. It was still unreal to me that I'd finally gotten the woman of my dreams. That was something I never expected to happen. That shit meant everything to me. Believe it or not, there were plenty of times that I found myself thanking God for bringing her into my life even though I didn't go to church or pray like I should.

"Why you looking at me like I'm a piece of meat?" she asked when she neared me. I wrapped my arms around her and pulled her into my lap. "Stop silly. I thought your leg was hurting."

"It is. If you kiss it, it'll make it all better," I teased.

"Nigga, ain't nobody about to suck your dick," she yelled and started giggling.

"You ain't gotta suck it. A little kiss not gonna hurt nobody," I commented and laughed.

Ding... Dong...

"Who the fuck is that?" I grunted. Just as I was about to get some, somebody rung the damn doorbell.

"I'll get it," Sia stated. I looked at her like she'd lost her damn mind. She knew damn well I didn't like for her to answer the door. I didn't give a damn if I wasn't at home and somebody rung it. It always came to my phone, so I could see who it was and what they wanted.

My *Ring* notification popped up on my phone. Sia picked it up and unlocked it. Yes, she had the password to my phone. There wasn't shit that I had to hide from her. That was a first for me. I've never trusted anyone that much, but she had that type of effect on me.

Zelle popped up on the screen. We unmuted the phone and told him to use his key to come in.

"I'll be back," I told Sia and put a t-shirt on. Sliding my feet in my Nike slides, I left out the room and met Zelle in the hallway. "Let's go to my office," I suggested. Zelle allowed me to lead the way.

"How you feeling?" he inquired.

"I'm good. What's going on with you? Why you out so late?" I replied. He looked drained. I'd never seen him look that way before. He didn't have to say much because I already knew that it had something to do with India

"You already know why. India had her crazy ass at the house trying to fuck and shit."

"And you didn't hit that?" I laughed.

"No. I'm pissed at her right now."

"For what?"

"You know how you told me she was going out. Well, I tracked her damn phone. Chucky drove me to where she was. I thought I might pull up on her, and maybe try and talk some sense into her, and get her to come home. But she had her ass out there with some burnt potato lookin' dude. I had to fuck the dude up from coming out of pocket with me. She stood there and tried to protect his ass.

That's what bothered me the most. Well, that and the fact that he said something to me about our relationship. How the fuck India gonna get with some random ass nigga and tell him what the fuck been going on in our relationship?" Zelle barked.

For me to say I didn't understand where he was coming from, would be a lie. This love shit cuts deeper than a mufucka when things don't go the way you want them to go. I knew that firsthand from the way things went with Sia and I.

"Listen... I'm new to this love thing, but I can understand how you're feeling. The shit between Sia and I was a rollercoaster ride I wasn't prepared to handle. One thing I learned was that trust and communication go a long way in a relationship."

"I know that. I trusted the fuck out of India until this shit with that nigga tonight. Ain't no telling what she told him about our relationship. In my mind, there is no reason for another nigga to be able to come to me about something concerning my woman. Just like she shouldn't have to worry about another woman coming to her about me."

"She may not have had to worry about it before, but since she got the video and picture of you with Pixie, you know it's going to take a while to regain her trust."

"I fucked up, Mon. I know that. Not one time did I deny it. She wouldn't even talk to me after she saw the shit. I understand she had a right to be mad, and she may have wanted space. But for her to start dating other people meant that our relationship was completely over. For that, she needs to leave me be. Of course, she came to the house and pulled the little stunt she pulled thinking I was gonna fuck her and everything would go back to normal."

"Hasn't that been the norm for y'all? One of you get mad at the other and you fuck each other's brains out and that's the end of that? You can't expect for her to think things would otherwise change if it's what you've been doing." I shrugged my shoulders. Look at me sounding like Dr. Phil and shit.

"I get it. I'ma talk to her, but I need some time to think. I asked her to leave and go back to her parents' house, and her ass tried to sneak to the other side of the house like I don't have cameras around the house and can see every damn thing. Plus, I never got a notification that a door had been opened, so it only made sense that she was still in the house."

Soon as he said that, Sia came in the room carrying my phone.

"Hey Zelle," she dryly spoke to him.

"Dang. I guess you spoke to India."

"Nope. But I don't like how things are with y'all, and I wish you would do whatever it takes to get her back." She rolled her eyes at him. On the inside I was laughing because her attitude could be so shitty at times, but on the outside, I kept a cool demeanor.

As they continued to talk, I looked at my phone. It was a notification for the alarm system that was in Zelle's house. I opened the app and my eyes damn near bulged out of my head.

"What's wrong?" Sia asked as I stood from behind my desk.

"We got to go," I told Zelle. He jumped up. That was one thing I could say about us. We never had to question one another when an order was given.

"What the fuck is going on?" Sia kept asking. I didn't want her to panic, so I told her that we needed to get to one of our traps.

"Let me go get my strap and I'll be right back." I handed Zelle my phone so he could see what I saw. Not once did I think about the fact that Sia was still standing there.

It took me less than five minutes to get my piece and head to the front door. Sia and Zelle had already left out the house.

"Where are you going?" I asked Sia.

"If this involves my best friend, then it involves me," she sternly stated. I shook my head. Arguing with her was not going to do anything but waste time. If she said she was going, I had no other choice but to let her go.

Chapter Ten:

Sianni

The video on Mon's phone showed Zelle and India's house in disarray. She'd never destroy her house like that because she loved everything about it. It was her safe haven.

"Stay put!" Mon demanded when we pulled into Zelle's driveway. The front door had been left wide open. They got out and ran inside the house screaming India's name.

Something about the entire situation didn't feel right to me. I looked at the doors and kept my eyes open in case I saw something out of the ordinary. The whole time they were inside the house, I had Mon's phone open following the cameras inside the house to see what was going on. From the looks of things, India was nowhere to be found.

Mon came running out to the car. I hit the unlock so he could get in.

"Call India's phone," he instructed me. I instantly dialed her number. All the phone did was ring. "Hopefully she was smart enough to grab it. Maybe we can track the phone." Mon suggested. That's when I looked up and saw

Zelle standing in the doorway holding up India's ringing phone.

"Fuck!" I bellowed. I was scared and mad at the same time. Who would take my best friend?

Zelle came out to the car and slid in on the passenger side. He grabbed Mon's phone and started reviewing the cameras from the time he left the house until the time Mon's phone got the alert. Plain as day, Link and Cynthia could be seen with a bunch of other men dressed in all black, grabbing India and the babies. For the first time since I'd met Zelle, I could tell he was visibly shaken. It was the first time that I'd ever seen tears sliding down his face.

"It's okay, Zelle. They are going to be okay." I tried my best to assure him. But he wasn't trying to hear anything I had to say.

"No, it's not. Had I not left her, then none of this shit would've happened. I don't even understand how they were able to get in the house anyways. I was sure I'd locked everything up and set the alarm before I left."

"Maybe she let them in. You never know," Mon stated.

"Or maybe they were already in the house and you didn't know it," I suggested.

Zelle looked at me and then went back to the phone. He rewound the video a little further back to before he got home with the babies. As sure as I said it, Link and Cynthia had taken their asses inside his home when he wasn't there. I'm not sure how they got in with his alarm on, but they were in his house the whole time, and he didn't know it.

"Fuck! How the hell could I be so damn stupid?" Zelle yelled while punching the dashboard.

"Let's take Sia back to the house. It's time that we finally handle this situation with Link and Cynthia," Mon expressed.

"Do what? No, the hell you aren't about to go after them. I just got you into my life, I don't want anything to happen to you," I cried.

"And what about India? She's your best friend or did you forget that?" Zelle roared.

"Don't do that. You know damn well that I love India, and would go through hell and high water to make sure she and my Godbabies were safe," I fussed.

"Then don't sit here and tell him that he can't help go after the bastard that has her. Stop being fuckin' selfish," Zelle snapped at me.

"Take me to my parents' house," I told Mon. I wasn't in the mood to be arguing with Zelle or no damn body else.

"I don't have time for that right now. I'm going to take you home so I can change. You can drive yourself to your parents' house," Mon told me. That angered me. Why wouldn't he just drive me to where I wanted to go? That was a sign that he'd pick Zelle over me if it ever came down to it.

"Whatever. Just take me home." It wasn't that I was being selfish. I was just worried about Mon. We'd just both been shot, and we were both still trying to fully recover from that. I didn't want him going out and possibly getting shot again. This time, he might not make it out alive.

"Go ahead and take her home. I need to go in here and get ready. Plus, the crew needs to be called. We are handling this shit tonight," Zelle barked. The look on his face said a lot. He got out the car and jogged back inside his house. Mon and I backed out of the driveway, and made our way back towards our house.

"I can't believe you don't want me to go after India and the babies," Mon spoke, breaking the silence between us.

"It's not that I don't want you to go after them."

"Then what is it?"

"It's the fact that I'm scared. I know what you do and that it was my choice to be with you after finding out what you do, but that doesn't mean that I want something happening to you. That shit that Tiny did to us has had me on high alert. Then the fact that Link and Cynthia were crazy enough to violate India and Zelle scares me more. What if you leave me here and they come grab me next?" I questioned him.

"Baby, I understand that. That's why I've decided to tell my Uncle Rocko that I'm not going to take over when he steps down. Once we find this money and get India and the kids back, I'm done with this street shit. You gave me a purpose to live the right way. I want us to have a family. The fact that you're carrying my seed lets me know that it's time for me to step away from this shit," he disclosed. Even though he tried to ease my worry, it didn't work.

Uncle Rocko didn't seem like the type of man that took no for an answer. How would he react once Mon told him that he was walking away from the shit? I just didn't want my baby to be hurt. Especially, with us about to be parents.

"We can talk about this more later. Let's just grab some stuff and get out of here. I texted your father on the way here, and he knows you're coming. You need to text me every ten minutes to let me know that you're okay while you're driving there. When you get there, you won't have to text me like that because I know that your father won't let anything happen to you. And please know that just because you're texting me, it doesn't mean I'm going to respond. It'll just help me to know that you're alright."

We got inside the house, and I packed an overnight bag while Mon got dressed. He was wearing all black, so I knew that meant somebody was about to get murdered. Silently, I prayed that he'd come back to me safely and in one piece.

"Stop staring at me like that." I was so involved in my thoughts, that I didn't realize I had been staring at him.

"Sorry," I apologized. He came over to me and wrapped his arms around me. I hugged him tight.

"Don't be sorry. I know you're worried, but don't be. I love you, and I want to spend the rest of my life with you and the little family we're going to have. I'm going to always come back to you."

"You promise?"

"I promise." He was hesitant in responding, so that didn't ease my worry much. At the end of the day, all I could do was take his word for it unless something proved otherwise.

"I hope you mean that. I don't want to go without you any longer."

"Believe me when I tell you that I feel the same way. Nothing in this world will ever keep us apart again," he advised me. I kissed him. It was one of the longest most passionate kisses we ever shared.

Mon slid on his black Timberland boots and we locked up the house. He walked me out to my car and reminded me of what he said about texting him and keeping him updated on where I was at. It was going to be hard for me to remember to text him, so I set my alarm to go off every ten minutes. He didn't need to be worried about me as much as he needed to worry about India and the babies. They were the only thing that he and Zelle needed to be concerned with at the moment. So, keeping in touch with him was not going to be anything that I fussed about.

Chapter Eleven:

India

It seemed like as soon as Zelle left out the door, the babies sensed it because they woke up crying. All three of them. That made me wonder what kind of bond he'd already built with them because they weren't that way whenever I would leave them alone.

Boom... Boom...

The sound of a loud noise caused me to stop in my tracks. Something was up. Zelle knew how I felt about our house, so he wasn't crazy enough to destroy anything.

Crash... Crash...

"What the fuck!!" I searched the room for my phone. It dawned on me that I'd left it in the guest room, so I had to either run to get the phone or go to the babies. At that point, the babies were more important. I hit the alarm keypad that was in our room so that Zelle and Mon would get an alert that something was wrong, and hightailed it towards the nursery.

"Not so fast." I heard as Link stepped out in front of me. "Where do you think you're going, sis?" He said with a wicked smirk on his face.

"She thought she was about to take my grandbabies, but that's not happening," Cynthia noted. I lunged at her ready to knock her neck off her shoulders, but Link caught me. I fought him as much as I could, but for some reason, I was really no match for his strength. Something had me feeling weak. I figured it had a lot to do with me worrying about my babies.

"Get her out of here," he ordered, and I suddenly felt my body being lifted off the floor. I was carried out of the house and thrown into the back of a van.

Not this shit again, I thought to myself. It was me thinking back to the time I was taken to Zelle. This shit had gotten ridiculous.

The sound of my babies crying could be heard loud and clear. I begged and pleaded for them to hand me my babies. A bag was thrown over my head and my hands and feet were tied together.

"You won't be getting them anytime soon," Link announced. "Y'all already know what to do with her," he told someone, and the van suddenly started moving.

The entire ride was done in silence. I called myself trying to listen out for any sounds that could indicate where I was at in case I found a way to reach out to Zelle. Unfortunately, they'd turned the music up so loud, I couldn't hear anything. By the time the van stopped moving, I found myself laid out on the floor, almost sleep. It seemed like we'd been riding forever, but I realized that the van made a lot of turns. It was almost as if they'd taken me in a circle to make it seem like we'd been driving a long distance.

"Wake up, sis. We're home," Link stated. The bag was removed from my head and I was pulled out of the van.

"Where the hell am I?" I asked as Link walked towards me.

"I said we're home. At least for now. Aren't you glad to be with your mother and brother?" I looked at him like he'd lost his mind. *Why the hell would I be happy to be around someone that just kidnapped me and that I'd just fuckin' came into contact with?*

Surveying my surroundings, it seemed like I was in the middle of nowhere. The house that was in front of me was rundown. There was a large field near it with tall glass. There wasn't another house in sight.

"Where are we?" I asked again.

"Stop asking so many damn questions about where you are. You act like I'm really going to tell you that. Trust me when I tell you that you'll figure it out soon enough," he told me. "We are about to be one big happy family."

At the mention of family, I realized that Cynthia and the babies were nowhere to be found. I began to panic. There wasn't much that I could do because my legs and arms were still tied together.

"Where's my babies?" I frantically asked.

"Don't you care enough to ask where our mother is?"

"Fuck that bitch! Where are my babies?"

"That's such a harsh thing to say about our mother."

Smack...

Without warning, Link smacked the fuck out of me.

"Untie my hands. I bet you won't smack me again," I told him.

"Now, why would I untie you so you can try to get away from me?"

"You don't have to worry about me trying to get away. You need to worry about me fuckin' you up. I've never let a man put his hands on me before, and I'm not about to start now," I cautioned him. That nigga fucked up when he put his hands on me, so I'd be more than happy to beat his ass.

"Oh, so little sis thinks she can really go toe to toe with her brother." He laughed. "Untie her," he advised one of the men.

The men laughed while I stood there thinking of ways I could capitalize on my current situation. The sad part about it was if I were to beat his ass, I still wouldn't be able to get away because I was very sure that the men he had with him would tie me back up.

"Stop looking so serious, sis. If you think you can beat me then you shouldn't have a worry in the world," he teased.

Bow...

As soon as my hands were set free, I punched him in the mouth. His smile quickly faded.

Biff... Biff... Bow...

Link gave me two swift punches to the stomach followed by an uppercut under my chin. I staggered a bit because I lost my footing. I was dizzy and thought I was going to fall. When I was able to see straight, I took off running towards him. I tackled him like a football player. He immediately fell to the ground, and I was on top of him. I delivered blow after blow to his face. All he did was lie there. He wasn't expecting me to beat his ass the way that I was, but I was fighting for not only my life, but the life of my babies.

"Get her off me," Link yelled, and the men pulled me off of him. They slung me over on the ground which gave him enough time to get up. Once he got up, I jumped up as well. I was getting ready to charge at him again, but was stopped.

Click... Clack...

The sound of him pulling out his gun, pointing it at me, and making sure a bullet went into the chamber was what stopped me.

"You not gonna keep putting your hands on me," Link yelled. He grabbed ahold of his bloody nose. It looked broke from where I was standing.

"Don't tell me you're afraid of lil' ole me," I snidely commented. "Put the gun down. You're acting like a bitch."

"Yeah, well you hit like a bitch," he told me.

"I hit like a bitch, yet you're the one with your shit broken and busted." I laughed at the sight of him spitting out blood.

"Fuck you," he yelled.

"Naw, I'm good. I don't fuck relatives. I did fuck you up, tho," I shrugged. "Now, where are my babies?"

"They are with our mother and as soon as I tell her what you did to me, you know you're probably never going to see your babies again," he babbled. What the fuck he say that for? I charged at his ass once more.

Link was ready for me this time. When I made it into his personal space, he hit me in the top of my head with the gun. I fell to the ground immediately. He straddled me and continuously hit me with the gun. He was so mad at the way I man handled him that he wanted to get revenge. What better way to do it than to pistol whip me?

Chapter Twelve:

Zelle

Mon and I went out looking for Link. The last known places we knew he'd been, he was not there. It was almost as if the nigga vanished off the face of the earth. Mon left me at his house to go out and grab something to eat. He thought it would be a good idea for us to eat and rest up before we came back to the table to make other plans on how we could locate Link's ass. We knew that if we found him, Cynthia wouldn't be too far away from his ass.

As soon as Mon left the house, I immediately called Chucky because he was one of the few people that could talk some sense into me. He and I went through the video over and over again and he provided me with an additional list of places he'd followed Link to. I ran up to the guest room I was supposed to be resting in to grab my boots while Chucky sat downstairs. I'd convinced him to take me back out to look for my family. There was no way I'd ever be able to sleep without knowing if they were safe or not.

"You ready?" he came in the room and asked me. I was sitting at the foot of the bed with my head resting in my hands. How could I be so stupid? With all the shit going on with Link, and after the way Tiny went after Sia and Mon, there was no reason that I shouldn't have had security detail on my family at all times.

None of this shit would've happened if I wouldn't have fucked with Pixie's trick ass. Had she not been killed the night I was shot, I would've put a bullet in that bitch's head myself. The way I felt, I could dig that bitch up and shoot the hoe just for the hell of it.

"Zelle, come on nigga. Snap out of it! We have to find your family," Chucky told me, tapping me on the shoulder.

"My bad. Let's go." By the time we made it downstairs, Mon was walking back inside the house.

"You know where we're going?" Mon asked Chucky. He knew me well enough to know that if I were going back out, it was because I had a lead. That's that brotherly shit right there. What was understood between us didn't need an explanation, right?

"Yeah. You wanna check some spots and we head to the others? That way we can kill some time." It made sense for us to split up, but something told me that we didn't need to do that.

"Let me see the list," I demanded. When Chucky handed it to me, I opened up Google Maps on my phone. I put in each individual address to see what the spots looked like. There had to be something that would lead us to them. There was no way we were going to have enough time to get through the entire list because it seemed that it would be something that Link wanted us to do. For some reason, I felt like he knew we had someone following him, so he was trying to lead us on a wild goose chase.

After looking at the list, there were a total of five houses that we singled out. It had a lot to do with their location and the way the houses looked. Link was smart enough to know not to go to his own crib because that would be the first placed that we checked. We didn't know of any other relatives they had and even if we did, he had to be smart enough to know not to go to them either. If Link thought the way that we did, then he would've known to go somewhere that we'd least expect to look. That was another reason that we narrowed it down to the five properties.

Staying together, the crew went from property to property, taking out any of his crew that was there and that could warn him that we were looking for him. We ransacked every last one of them and took all of the drugs and money that he had there as well. That was definitely going to piss his ass off and if we were lucky, it would flush his ass out of hiding if we didn't find him soon.

We'd rode around for at least three hours. The crew had started to get tired. Even Mon dosed off a time or two. It was late and we should've taken some time to rest, but I couldn't. There was so much adrenaline running inside of me that there was no way I could sleep. How could I?

After another hour, we came to one of the houses that had a *Scooby-Doo* like van parked out in front of it. I shook Mon to wake him up. It had to be the house we'd been looking for.

"Get up, nigga. This has to be the one," I told him. I was sure of it because there were two men standing outside by the front door, and we could see a few more standing strategically around the house.

"Are you sure?" Mon asked me.

"Just look," I told him. Pointing at the men that were around it. "Pull in the driveway."

Chucky pulled in the driveway as I said, followed by the other two Suburbans that contained the rest of the crew members that we had tag along with us. There was no reason for us to try to be discreet because there was nowhere for us to hide the vehicles and try to sneak up on them.

The men started shooting at the Suburbans, but they were wasting their bullets because they were bulletproof. We sat in the vehicles giving them time to get as many bullets out as they could and when they had to change their clips, that was when we made our moves. We came out all guns blazing. Nobody was safe.

Once the men that were outside were taken care of, Mon and I entered the house behind Chucky and a few other men. There were a total of ten men in the living room with their guns out, including Link.

"I wouldn't start shooting if I were you. Your girl and kids are in here somewhere," Link spoke. I lifted my hand so my men knew not to shoot. I'd never be able to forgive myself if the people I loved were hurt because I was careless.

"Where are they?" I asked. There was no reason for me to beat around the bush with my questions because we all knew why we were there.

"Where is who?" Link replied, trying to play dumb.

"Nigga, don't play with me. Where the fuck is my family?" I roared.

"Oh, them... They're around." Link was taunting me, and I couldn't take it. The shit had to end, and it had to end soon.

Turning to face Chucky and Mon, I nodded my head. They all knew what that meant. We all angled our bodies to where we had certain men in front of us. We lifted our guns and started shooting. Within a matter of seconds, all of Link's men were laid out on the floor dead. Link stood there like he'd seen a ghost. He was not ready for the heat we brought to him. I'd be scared too if I were him. The sad part was he'd depended so much on his men to keep him safe, that his ass wasn't prepared for what we'd done.

"Check the rest of this place out. We have to find my family," I ordered. Everyone in the crew scattered to different parts of the house. The only two left standing in the living room were Link and I. He tried to remain composed, but I could see him trembling like a hoe in church.

"if you kill me, you'll never see your family again," he threatened me.

"That's where you're wrong. We run these streets. When we want something to happen, it does. You can keep playing with me if you want. I promise you're only going to make things worse for you and your baldheaded ass bitch of a momma," I barked.

"Bingo," Mon yelled out. "I need you guys to get in here fast," he continued. The men came flying past me and into the direction of Mon's voice.

"What is it?" I yelled out.

"I found our missing money."

"That's not your money. That's my shit and you better leave every penny there," Link quipped.

"And if we don't? What are you going to do from the grave?"

"You wouldn't kill me because India would never forgive you. Cynthia and I are the only real family that she has. There's no way she'd let you kill us."

"Luckily for me, India's not here. I can always tell her that someone else took your ass out. She'd believe me because I'm sure you have more enemies than me."

"She'd never go for that."

"Well, that's a risk I'm willing to take," I informed his ass and I meant every word of that.

"Go get the suitcases out the car and start loading the shit up. Put all the drugs in the trash bags," I instructed.

Link already looked like someone had fucked him up, but that didn't stop me from beating his ass some more. While the crew was moving the money and drugs out the house, I had fun boxing Link's ass out. He tried his best to be a match for me, but he didn't stand a chance. It wasn't until Mon came back and told me that they had everything out the house that I stopped beating the shit out of Link.

"Was there any sign of India or the kids?" I asked Mon. He simply shook his head. "If you did something to hurt my family, I promise you will not like what happens to you. Now, tell me where they are!" I roared.

Link stood there smiling. He acted as if I didn't say anything to him. I'd had more than enough of his presence. I was ready to dismiss his ass permanently. Lifting my gun, I walked up to Link and pressed it against his forehead. Mon came over and whispered in my ear for me to chill out. He wanted a chance to question Link, to see if he could find out the real reason he'd been fuckin' with us and India. As bad as I wanted to tell him fuck no and go ahead and end Link's life, I couldn't. He was the only one that could lead us to India and the babies, so I really had no choice but to let Link live a little while longer.

Chapter Thirteen:

R'Mondo

We were in an intense standoff with Link. Our crew had taken out everyone that was a part of his crew. Zelle wanted to kill Link as soon as we saw him, but I had to stop him. Something about the entire situation seemed off to me. There was no way Link would come after us just because we wouldn't put him on. What sense did that make? Then, he had too many people working for and with him to pull off the shit that he'd done. There was something we were missing.

"I'm not about to keep playing around with this nigga. We let him get away one too many times already. I'm not letting him go out that door unless it's in a body bag," Zelle roared.

"I agree with you, but we have to figure out what the fuck is going on," I asserted.

"What the fuck you mean? This nigga took my girl and kids. That's all we need to know," Zelle grunted. He was stubborn as fuck, so when he'd made his mind up about something, it was hard to get him to change it. Killing Link was the only thing on his mind. No one could blame him for that because Link had been on some foul shit from the moment we laid eyes on him. I still wanted to know why?

"I didn't say you weren't going to kill him because I agree with you... The only way he will be leaving is when his body drops for the last time. Just think about the shit, Zelle. This nigga has to be working with or for someone. None of the shit he's done has added up," I tried to explain.

"Yeah, he's working with that Cynthia bitch, and you better believe that when I lay eyes on her, I'm killing her ass too."

"Who sent you?" I turned to a battered Link. Someone had clearly busted his ass before we arrived.

"Fuck all that! Where is my girl and my kids?" I threw my hand up to stop Zelle. He was going about things the wrong way, and if he didn't stop, we'd never get what we wanted out of Link.

"Don't look at him, look at me," I told Link. "Why have you been coming after us?"

"You're right, I have been working with someone. It's because of you that he lost everything."

"He who? Who sent you?"

"Why does it matter who sent me?"

"Link, you are in no position to play games with us. If you don't quit bullshitting me, I'm going to turn Zelle loose on your ass," I warned him.

"Who said I was playing games with you? I'm telling your ass the truth."

"Why did you come after India? How the fuck did you switch from coming after us to going after my girl?" Zelle finally asked a logical question.

"My mother and I was always going to come for India. That part had nothing to do with either of you," Link spoke.

"Why? Why were you coming for her? That bitch gave my baby away. There was no reason for her to come after her for anything," Zelle grunted.

"My mother had every reason to come after India. It was because of India that our lives changed forever. Had she never been born, my mother would be further in life than she is and we would've had so much."

"What the fuck is that supposed to mean? If you're twins, then that should mean you were as big of a problem as India was. Why keep one and not the other? That's stupid as fuck."

"You asked me a question and I'm giving you the answer. I'm not going to go into any more detail then that because it's my mother's story to tell. At the end of the day, just know that when we decided to come after India, someone found out about it. They gave my mother and I a proposition to take the two of you out; then I can be on top in these streets. I was made to be the King of these streets and y'all have been standing in my way," he explained.

"Who sent you?" I asked him again. "Fuck all that other shit you rambling about."

"You'll never get that out of me."

"Fine! We don't have any other reason to keep your ass alive," I advised him. "Go ahead and kill him, Zelle."

"You're a fuckin' lie. He needs to tell me where my girl and kids are," Zelle stated. "Now, tell me where the fuck they are!" How the hell this nigga was just about to kill his ass but now he standing here telling me to wait? I ran my hand down my face because Zelle was starting to confuse the fuck out of me. I had no choice but to back him up.

"Tell us who the fuck you have been working for all this time," I added.

"Fuck both y'all niggas. I'm not telling you shi-"

Pow... Pow... Pow... Pow... Pow... Pow... Pow... Pow... Pow...

Link didn't get a chance to finish his statement. Zelle emptied his clip on his ass. It was inevitable that Link was going to be killed, but it was at the wrong time. We didn't get all the answers that we needed. Where was India? Where were the babies?

"Aye, I need y'all to come see something," Chucky told us when he stepped inside the room we were in.

"What is it?" Zelle asked.

"Just bring your ass on," Chucky returned. He started jogging to the back of the house and we jogged right behind him.

Chucky led us through the kitchen and out the backdoor. There was an old rundown shed out there. Some of the crew were standing right outside of it, waiting for us to get there.

"Go in," Chucky instructed us as we reached the shed. Zelle and I looked at each other before making sure our guns were out and ready to fire. We stepped inside the shed and there sat India hogtied on the floor with her mouth duct-taped.

Zelle ran to India and began untying her. The only thing I could do was stand there in awe. India looked like she'd been in the ring with a UFC fighter. If Link wasn't already dead, he'd be fucked after this shit. I'd already put it on my mind that Zelle was not going to stop until everybody behind India being hurt and the babies being missing were sent to their grave.

Chapter Fourteen:

Sianni

The whole time I was at my parents' house, I kept texting Mon to see if he was okay and if they found India. It worried me because he didn't respond. It was like he kept his phone on to give me time to get to my parents' house then he ghosted me once I told him I made it.

"You need to try to get some rest," my father came into the living room and told me to go to my room so that I could get some rest, but I couldn't. My nerves were all over the place.

"I am, daddy. I'm just worried."

"There's nothing to be worried about. Mon and Zelle have been running these streets for a long time. They know what they're doing."

"Wait... How did you know what he did?"

"You must've forgotten that your dad used to be the man in these streets. Even though I stepped away from it because shit had gotten too bad, that doesn't mean I don't know what's going on. Plus, the minute I laid eyes on Mon and Zelle, I knew what they were about," he admitted.

"Does that mean you don't want me to be with him? I don't want this to be another one of those situations where you don't approve, and we end up at odds about it. You know how things went with Yosef."

"Sia, Mon and Yosef are on two different levels. Mon is like steak and Yosef is like dogfood. I'm sure you can tell the difference." I couldn't help but laugh at the way he'd compared the two. "I'm being serious, Sia. I love you, and I'll always have your best interest at heart. Yosef was not good for you. I tried to accept him when you first came home with him. But after awhile, it was hard to do. He was doing shit to you that even I wouldn't tolerate and making excuses about it as if he weren't in the wrong. He wanted you to act like he was this perfect boyfriend and we all knew that he wasn't. There were plenty of times I wanted an excuse to put my foot up his ass. However, I understand you are a grown woman, and I have to let you make your own decisions. Even when you fall down behind those decisions, I'll always be there to catch you and help you back up," he told me. That made me start crying.

My father and I have always had the best relationship. I actually had a good relationship with both of my parents, but I was the true definition of a daddy's girl.

"When I told you that I would get things changed in your inheritance, I was going to do it because it would be in your best interest. Yosef was using you and bringing you down, and you're too good of a woman for me to stand back and let that happen. Mon knows that you can hold your own. He hasn't treated you bad, and he holds you accountable for anything you do wrong. That's the same way I am with your mother. It doesn't mean we love you any less, it just means that we expect more from you because we know the amount of greatness that's inside of you. Do you understand?" I nodded my head to let him know that I did. "Good. Now, tell me when you started fuckin' him and if that is his child because if it belongs to Yosef, we gotta go get rid of it."

The look on my face was one that I'm sure he'd never seen before. Did he really just tell me that he'd want me to abort my baby if it belonged to Yosef?

"Chill out, Sia. I'm only playing with you. I don't care about your sex life at all. However, I can tell that Mon be hitting those switches right because your ass walks with a new rhythm. You glow and you seem so much happier now. I'm happy that you've found happiness. But you need to know this..." He paused.

"Okay..." I waited for him to say what he was about to say.

"These streets ain't no joke. There will be bitches who will try to test you. They'll lie and say they're fuckin' your man and couldn't point his dick out in a lineup. Don't allow those bitter hoes to come between you and your man. Trust him unless he gives you a reason not to. Always keep the lines of communication open even when it seems like something too hard to talk about. Remain honest in everything that you do. If he asks you if you farted and you know you did, tell his ass. It may be embarrassing but tell him anyway. Shit that's a normal body function, and I'm sure his fart will blow your ass across the street," he chuckled.

"Really daddy?"

"What? I was trying to get you to smile." I giggled a bit because he was crazy. One thing I loved about my father was the fact that I could talk to him about any and everything and I could trust that he would be completely honest with me no matter if it'd hurt my feelings or not.

"Take heed to what he's telling you about these dusty hoes because they will try you. Even if they give you receipts, don't ever let them see you sweat. But if Mon is anything like your father, when he fucks up, he'll tell you. There was never a time that a bitch could come to me and tell me anything about your dad that he hadn't already told me. He tried me a few times, but when I almost cut his dick off, he got some act right," my mother came from around the corner and chimed in on our conversation. That's when I really fell out laughing. My father sat there looking crazy as hell.

"Don't get quiet now. Momma had you scared, huh?"

"Hell yeah and to this day, I still don't cross the line with another bitch or even do anything to make your mom have the slightest thought that I'm fuckin' up because she's my world. I'd die if I lost her or you. I can tell that Mon is going to be the same way about you and the baby," my father spoke. That reminded me that I didn't answer his question about the father of my child.

"By the way, Mon is the father. I'm not sure what I would've done if I even thought Yosef was the father," I admitted.

"Are you sure?" my mother asked.

"Yes, I'm positive. I used my period tracker to keep up with when I had my cycle, and I also notated when I had sex with Mon. I've only had a half session of sex with Yosef since dealing with Mon, and we never even finished, so I can assure you that Mon is the father of my child." My mother started doing a praise dance to be funny. All I could do was laugh.

My phone started ringing. I'd had it on the side table so that it could charge.

"I'll pass it to you," my mother told me since she was already standing up. It was Mon finally calling back.

"Hello baby," I greeted him.

"Meet me at the hospital that India gave birth at," Mon instructed and hung up the phone without giving me the chance to respond.

"Oh, my God! Something's wrong with Mon. He just told me to meet him at the hospital," I cried. My mother and father ran to the room and came out ready to go.

"Get your ass up so we can go," my father told me. I went to the back to grab my purse.

All I had on was a sports bra, some shorts that stopped a little under my ass, and some fuzzy house shoes. I was so worried about Mon that I didn't bother to stop and change. I threw a big hoodie on to hide my sports bra and ran right out of the room.

"Let's go," I told my parents.

Running out the door, my father beat me to the car. They were going to drive me because they knew how I was when I was worried. I panicked a lot and became paranoid. It was not safe at all for me to drive like that, so them driving me wasn't an issue at all. Plus, I felt like I was going to need their support. With everyone in the car, we made our way towards the hospital. I prayed the entire time we were in the car.

Chapter Fifteen:

R'Mondo

With Link dead, there was a weight lifted off my shoulders. It wasn't a huge amount of weight, but it was enough to bring me some comfort. He mentioned that his real intentions were to come after India for ruining their lives, but informed us that he was paid to come after Zelle and me instead. Zelle killed him before I could get to the bottom of what was really going on. I wasn't mad at him because the issues he was dealing with were a lot. He was frustrated and no one could blame him for that.

India was hurt pretty badly when we got to her. Her breathing was shallow, and she was battered and bruised. I told Zelle and Chucky to roll out to the hospital while I made sure our money and the drugs got somewhere safe. We couldn't take all that shit to the hospital with us because we knew the medical staff were going to ask questions about what happened to India and would more than likely call the police if they didn't like the explanation that was given to them.

As soon as Zelle and Chucky pulled away with India, we searched the house once more to see if there was anything else we could find and possibly look for something that could suggest where Cynthia had gone with the babies. We cleared out any and everything that we felt could be valuable. I made it a point to take Link's phone. He had an iPhone 8, so his thumb print could be used to unlock the phone. I cut his fuckin' thumb off, stuck it inside a Wal-Mart bag and stuck the bag in my pocket. I was going to look inside the phone when I got around Zelle and he was ready to do it.

"We got everything?" I asked the crew to be sure. When they told me we did, I stepped outside and called the clean-up crew.

Peanut and Junebug were the two niggas riding in the car with me. They'd been around for a while, so we felt as though we could trust them. I had them take me to one of the houses that Zelle and I used to hide money at. The rest of the crew headed on up to the hospital with Zelle and India.

We got to the house and pulled straight up under the garage. I had Peanut and Junebug help me carry everything that we collected inside the house. We went straight to the basement where we had a vault built inside.

The guys had to stay upstairs until I used our secret code to open the vault and when it was open, I had them neatly sit everything inside of the vault. They were in awe at what they'd seen. There was so much money inside the vault that you'd think we owned our own damn bank.

Once everything was unloaded, he headed towards the hospital as well. I called Sia on the way and told her to meet me at the hospital that India delivered the triplets at. Although I knew she was probably worried, I couldn't give out too much information over the phone.

As usual, we arrived at the hospital and went directly to the waiting area. The whole crew was in there worried about India. Zelle looked a mess. We all needed baths and some rest, but we couldn't rest until we found the babies and Cynthia was off the streets like Link. It was going to be a matter of time before she realized that his life had come to an end. Maybe when she did find that out, she'd be smart enough to release the babies. That could've spared her from some of the torture Zelle was going to put on her ass.

"Have you heard anything?" I asked Zelle as I gave him a bro hug.

"She was beat up pretty badly. She was resting, so I didn't want to go in and disturb her. Especially, since I know she's going to ask me about the babies, and I don't have an answer for her."

"Stop beating yourself up over this. You could've had a crew outside watching her and things still could've went wrong. Link was out to get us and prove a point and he did it the best he could even though we still came out on top. We are going to get the babies back; don't worry."

"What you do with the merchandise?" he asked. I knew he was trying to change the subject as a way to ease his mind, so I followed his lead.

"I took it to the crib." He already knew what that meant so there was no need for me to say anything else.

"Aight. Cool."

"Oh, my God! Baby, what happened? Are you okay?" Sia came running inside the waiting room. She came straight towards me and used her hands to roam all over my body. "What happened? Are you okay?" she asked again.

"I'm fine. We found India," I advised her.

"Okay, where is she?"

"She was beat up pretty badly, but she's going to be fine," Zelle informed her.

"Can we see her?" she questioned. That's when I allowed my eyes to survey her sexy ass body.

"Come here," I told her. Grabbing her by the hand, I pulled her inside the family restroom that was in the waiting area. I made sure to lock the door behind us.

"What's wrong? Is there something you couldn't tell me in front of them?" she asked, pointing towards the lobby.

"What the fuck you got on, Sia? I know damn well you know better than that," I fussed.

"Really Mon? This is ignorant as hell and not the time for us to be arguing over something dumb."

"Yes, really! Now what the fuck are you wearng?"

"Mon, I was at home trying to rest when you called. This was what I was wearing. I was so worried that I ran on out of the house. I didn't have time to change clothes," she explained.

"Don't do that shit again. I don't want these thirsty ass niggas eyeing my woman down."

"Mon, I could've worn a damn trash bag and there would still be all eyes on me. Stop sweating the little shit because you know everything on this body belongs to you."

"Is that so?" I probed, sucking on my bottom lip. Her ass was sitting right in those lil' ass shorts.

"We don't have time for that Mon."

"Shittin' me. Watch this shit."

Pulling my pants down, I allowed my dick to spring up. He was ready for action.

"Stop playing, Mon," she insisted.

Without warning, I flipped her around and bent her over the sink. Pulling her shorts down, I allowed them to slide down to her ankles before I found myself inside of her love tunnel.

"Mmmm..." she moaned the minute she felt me inside of her. Slowly, I glided in and out of her wet pussy. That shit felt so amazing. I took my time because I didn't want it to end.

Glancing up into the mirror, I kept my eyes trained on hers. We were in our own little head space as we kept gazing into each other's eyes.

"Damn Mon... You 'bout to make me cum already," she expressed.

"Go ahead and let that shit go. I'm about to bust all inside of you, Sia."

Not even five minutes later, she was loudly moaning as she came all on my dick. Feeling her juices raining down on my dick made me cum right after her."

With my head rested on her back, we spent a few moments just standing there.

"I needed that shit, baby. I can't wait until this is all over so I can really go home and make love to you."

"It's coming baby. Don't worry about that," I assured her.

Knock... Knock...

"Bring y'all nasty asses out of there," Zelle hollered.

Sia and I used some papertowels to clean ourselved up before rejoining everyone in the waiting room. As soon as we opened the bathroom door, everybody was staring at us and smiling.

"Fuck y'all," I cracked.

"Zelle, what room is India in? I want to go see her," India advised him.

"She's in room 5149. You gon' back there and I'll be back there shortly. We're trying to figure out how we're going to find the babies," Zelle advised her.

"What do you mean by that? Weren't they with her?"

"You're asking too many questions, Sia. You know how this shit goes. We can talk about this later. Go check on India," I told her. Sia worked my nerves asking all those damn questions, but I understood that it came with her being concerned about the people she loved.

"I'm going to go back there too. I don't want India to wake up and think I left her hanging," Zelle announced.

"I get it, man. I'ma step outside with the crew and see what we can come up with to get the babies back. Don't worry, we got you."

"Yeah, we got you," they all said in unison. Zelle let out a small smile. That was better than nothing.

As soon as Zelle was out of sight, I stepped outside with the crew. I told them to go home and get a couple of hours of rest because we were about to tear these streets up looking for Cynthia and the triplets. The outcome was probably going to be bloody and there may be a few innocent people who lose their life a long the way, but we were going to do what needed to be done by any means necessary.

Chapter Sixteen:

India

My body was hurting all over. Fighting with Link may not have been the best thing for me to do. At the time, it seemed right. Now, I wish I would've just gone along with whatever he told me to do.

Lying in my hospital bed, I stared up at the ceiling. Medical staff kept coming in and out of the room, but I didn't have anything to say to any of them.

Knock... Knock...

There were two knocks on the door before it flew open and in walked Sia. I smiled because I was happy to see her.

"Awwww... Sis, I'm sorry this happened to you. How are you feeling?" she asked me.

"Like I was hit by a Mack truck. Have they found the babies?"

"Not yet, but they will. Don't worry because you know they'll get to them just like they got to you." I knew that Zelle and Mon were going to do everything in their power to get the babies home safely, but I still couldn't help but worry. They were with Cynthia and from experience, I knew that Cynthia was not the type of person that dealt with kids. You saw what her dumb ass did to me.

"What happened to Link?" I asked Sia as if she knew.

"I don't know. They won't tell me much of anything, but I'm sure it wasn't a good thing."

"No, it wasn't," Zelle muttered as he walked through the door. He came right over to the bed and kissed me on the forehead. "I'm sorry, India. All of this shit is my fault. Had I kept my dick in my pants, you never would've been hurt." I appreciated the fact that Zelle apologized. That was all I really wanted from him anyways.

"It's not your fault. I should've listened to you when those pictures came through. It was clear that the only reason they sent the shit to me was to ruin our special day and I allowed it to happen. We promised each other that we'd talk to each other when we had an issue and instead of me staying true to that, I pushed you away. Then I went out on a date to make you jealous. I was never going to move on. I just wanted you to feel the way I felt when I saw you with another woman. That was my dick and you let another bitch feel it." Just saying those words brought tears to my eyes.

Zelle climbed in the bed with me. It hurt me a little for him to touch me, but I didn't say anything because I wanted him near me. I needed to feel him because he made me feel safe.

"I know this is going to be hard, but can you tell me what happened," he commented. "Who the hell beat up Link?" I started laughing. Even that hurt, but I couldn't help myself. "Wait... Did you do that?" Zelle sat up and asked me.

"Yeah, I beat the shit out of him. The only reason I got all these bruises on me is because he wasn't a match for me. He pistol whipped me." I laughed but Zelle stopped.

"I'ma kill his ass," Zelle bellowed.

"You already did," Mon spoke as he walked inside the room.

"Damn, people don't know how to knock anymore?" I joked.

"Bitch, I know you lying. I knocked twice before I came in here," Sia giggled. It was hurting me so bad to laugh, but I needed those laughs.

"What about the babies?" I looked at Zelle and asked. He shook his head no to tell me that he hadn't found them yet. It was draining him physically and emotionally. I could tell by his demeanor.

"What happened India?" Mon asked her.

"Zelle and I got into it. I was in the house crying about it and trying to figure out how I could make things right when I heard these loud noises. I thought about my cell phone, but I'd left it on the opposite end of the house. That's when I decided I needed to get to the kids. I hit the button on the alarm in the room so it could send an alert to y'all phone and ran towards the nursery. By the time I reached the nursery, Link was there with Cynthia. They tied me up and threw me in the back of a van. I could've sworn that I heard the babies in the van with me, but when we started moving, I didn't hear them anymore. It wasn't until I got to that house that I realized that they'd separated me from the babies."

"How did you and Link get to fighting?" Sia probed.

"He was talking shit and he smacked me when I said something smart to him. I told him to untie me and I'd beat his ass. He didn't think I'd fight him, so he had his guys untie me. I started beating his ass and he was so embarrassed that he pistol whipped me." I smiled once more. I was proud of the beating I put on his ass. "I know y'all think I'm crazy for laughing about it, but that's the only thing I could say was good about this shit. Laughing is what's keeping me from breaking down and crying. I wouldn't be good for the babies if I was a nervous wreck."

"When you leave from here, you're going home with Sia and her parents. I've already talked to her father about it and he has no problem with it. He can keep the two of you safe until we handle this shit with Cynthia," Zelle announced. I looked at him like he was crazy as hell. There was no way I was going to let him be out there looking for our kids and I'm sitting on my ass not doing shit.

"That's not going to happen. I'm going to help," I chided.

"You're going to help by sitting your ass at the house with Sia and letting me and Mon handle this shit. You're not about to have me out here worrying about you when

I'm already worried about them. Now, I know you like to be stubborn and hardheaded, but this is one time that I really need your ass to do what I'm saying," Zelle snapped. I knew he wasn't trying to be mean, so there was no reason for me to say anything smart to him. It was time that I learned to sit my ass down and let my man take the lead. If he said that he got it, I have to trust him enough to believe that he really does have it.

"Okay, I'll leave it alone. But I want you to promise that you're going to keep me posted on your every move," I told him. He said he was fine with doing that. Hearing him say that did make me feel a little better, but I wouldn't be all the way better until my babies were back at home with us, where they were supposed to be.

"The doctor said they just wanted to keep you overnight to make sure you were okay. They are going to send you home with some pain medication and some cream to put on the marks so that it won't leave bruises on your body. I think Sia is going to stay the night with you tonight and I'm going to head to the house. I have to meet up with the crew just so we can plan out what we're going to do next," Zelle informed me.

"I already talked to them. I'll let you know what's up once we get from out of these walls," Mon stated.

"Aight. Bet. Where the crew?"

"I told them to go home and get some rest. These next twenty-four hours are going to be hell," Mon stated.

"I know. I'ma go home and get a shower and try to get a few hours of sleep in as well," Zelle told me.

"Yeah, me too," Mon cosigned.

"You need me to come take a nap with you, Mon?" Sia asked. She winked at him, so I knew what that meant.

"Naw. Stay your freaky ass right there. I'ma give you some dick when we get the babies back."

"But I can't sleep without it," she whined. I couldn't help but laugh at her. She sounded like me when I had to beg Zelle for some dick. Those niggas know they can be stingy at times.

"Girl, bye!" Mon told her. "I just gave you a quicky in the bathroom, so you'll be fine," he continued. He went over and gave her a hug and a kiss. "Sis, I'm going to check on you tomorrow. Please listen to what Zelle asked you to do and don't go out there trying to be superwoman."

"Wait... before you leave, I want to say something. The house that Link took me too, that was the house that my mother grew up in. It was the very house that her parents put her out of. She would take me to visit them all the time. They would be nice to me, but whenever she wanted them to babysit or to buy me things, they would tell her no. When they died, she went back to live in that very house. That was the house that I last remembered living in before she dropped me off."

"If your mother had you and Link at the same time, why is it that you don't remember him? She kept you until you were six. Surely, you would've remembered if you had a brother."

"You'd think I would because I can remember other shit, but not that. I'd never seen a little boy in our presence. I'm not even sure if they were truthful in saying that Link was my twin brother. And if he was, where the fuck did she hide him at? None of this adds up and I know we won't find out the answers until we're able to find Cynthia."

"Cynthia seems to be the missing piece of the puzzle. She may also be the person that can let us in on who hired them to try to get rid of us," Mon chimed in.

"Huh? What do you mean by that?" I asked.

"Link told us some shit before we sent him home." I knew he meant before they killed his ass, so I just looked at him when he made his statement. "Anyways, he said that him and Cynthia came back to get revenge on you and when someone learned what they were doing, they told him that they'd pay him to get rid of Zelle and I. He never told us who the person was. I believe that Cynthia may be able to tell us more. Especially, since Zelle allowed him to go home before I could get as much as I could out of him," Mon grunted.

"He should've kept his fuckin' hands to himself then," Zelle replied. We all laughed at how serious Zelle was. His ass was sitting there talking like they were in preschool or some shit.

"I got it, bruh," Mon told him. "We will let y'all in on everything once we get out of here," Mon assured me. That was fine by me. I just wanted them to do what they had to do to bring my babies home.

The men left out of the room and Sia and I were the only ones left. Her parents went home and told us that they would come get us early in the morning.

"Are you sure you're okay, sis?" Sia asked me.

"Yes, I'm fine. I'm in a little pain, but that's to be expected after the night I had," I responded to her.

"Girl, tell me again how you beat his ass," Sia stated. We laughed as I told her the story blow by blow. The shit was funny. Nobody couldn't say that it wasn't. For me to have beat the shit out of Link and the fact that I was a woman said a lot. Zelle had better watch his back the next time he decides he's going to fuck up.

Chapter Seventeen:

Zelle

"Aye, you gon' to the waiting room and I'll be right back," I told Mon. "I'll send Sia to join you."

"You bout to get some pussy. You not fooling me," Mon commented.

"Nobody said that when you had Sia in the bathroom hollering like a wounded dog."

"Fuck you!" I said and pushed his ass into the wall.

"I got you, bro. Send Sia's ole whining ass out here. I'ma take her back in the bathroom," he advised me. I couldn't do shit but laugh.

"Aight. Bet." I dapped him up and headed back into India's room. The girls were lying in her bed laughing hard as hell.

"What's wrong, baby?" India asked me.

"I needed to show you something. Sia can you excuse us? Mon is waiting for you in the hall."

"Oooooo..." Sia spoke.

"What's wrong?" India probed.

"You bout to get somet dick, bitch! You better get that shit," Sia teased. She stood up and started twerking. Her ass was crazy as fuck but you couldn't help but to love her.

"Bye Sia!" I told her, trying my best to hold my laugh in.

"Fine. Lemme go try to get another qucky in. I'll holla."

Sia left the room and I immediately came out of my pants, boxers, and boots. Sliding under the covers with India, we both turned on our sides. Lifting her gown up, I noticed she didn't have any panties on.

Smack...

"What the fuck!" she exclaimed. "Why the fuck you smack me that hard?"

"Where the fuck your panties at?"

"You must've forgotten how the hell I was when you left the house. The only thing I had time to throw on was a damn gown." When she reminded me what she'd been through, I felt bad.

"I'm sorry, baby. You know how I am about your body."

"How is that?" she asked.

"Like this..." I said and slid right inside of her. That shit felt so good that I almost busted right then. I had to think about Link's ass to keep from nutting so fast.

"Damn Zelle. I missed this shit," India told me.

"I missed it too. I'm so sorry baby. I never meant to hurt you. When I told you that I was going to spend the rest of my life making that shit up to you, I meant that. Please don't ever leave me again. I was lost without you." The whole time I spoke, I was still stroking inside of her from behind.

"Oh, my God! You're so deep, Zelle," she whined.

"That's because I'm trying to give you another baby," I replied. She started bucking like I knew she would. I grabbed ahold of her waist and held her tightly so she couln't move so much. I kept delivering long deep strokes inside of her.

"I'm cumin', Zelle. Fuckkkkkk..." she exclaimed. I kept fuckin' her as she reached her peak. Her body did a slight slump as I kept pumped. Five minutes later, it was time for me to explode.

"Ssssss..." I hissed as I allowed all of my seeds to flow inside of her.

"I love you, Zelle and I'm sorry for hurting you too. I swear that I'll never leave you ever again. No matter what happens, it'll never be something we can't get through together," she assured me. She turned to face me and we ended up engaging into a passionate kiss. Our tongues were doing a dance of their own inside each other's mouth.

Knock... Knock...

"Y'all hoes not done yet?" Sia opened the door and asked.

"Yes, bitch! Now, get out so my baby can get dressed."

"Aight. I'ma go get some disinfectant spray and find the housekeeper. Ain't no way I'm sleeping on those sexed out sheets," she joked and shut the door. That's when I got up and went into the bathroom.

Soaping up a towel, I cleaned myself and put my clothes on before I went to clean India. I kissed her once more and waited for Sia to return to the room before I left.

"Call me on Sia's phone if you need anything," I told them before joining Mon in the hallway so we could leave the hospital.

Mon and I went back to his place to get some rest. I said I was going to go home, but I didn't. I couldn't because of the shit that had went down there. The only thing I would've done was continue to watch the video footage of what happened inside the house and think about ways I wanted to kill Cynthia's ass once my babies were safe.

"You want to stop and grab something to eat?" Mon asked me.

"Naw. I'm good. I just want to lay down for a while."

"You sure because I can hear your stomach growling," he told me. I laughed because I heard the shit too. We decided to stop at Krystal's which was a drive thru that stayed open 24/7. The line was long as hell, so we had to wait a while. I felt myself dozing off while we sat there and waited. It seemed like we were there forever, but Mon told me it had only been twenty minutes.

We ate on our way back to his house. I should've had him stop by my house, so I could've grabbed some fresh clothes, but that was going to be out of the way. When we made it to Mon's house, I went to the guest room that India and I always stayed in when we visited them. As soon as my body hit the bed, I was out cold.

***

When I woke up, my body felt sore as hell. I was sluggish and didn't want to get out of bed. The only reason I got up was because I smelled food being cooked. I dragged myself out the bed and went inside the bathroom that was adjoining the bedroom. Interestingly, I noticed there were a fresh set of clothes and some hygiene items. I'm not sure where the stuff came from, but I was thankful to have it.

The first thing I did was step in the shower. All I had on was hot water because I knew it would help my sore and fatigued body feel better. I stayed in there until the water started to turn cold and that's when I started to take my bath. I got out and put on the clothes that were laid out for me and brushed my teeth.

It took me a minute to want to face anybody, but I finally left out of the room and headed straight for the kitchen. I was shocked to find Sia, India, Sia's parents, and Mon in the kitchen.

"What the hell are you doing here, India?" I roared. I didn't have time for her ass to be hardheaded.

"She asked to come see you and so we brought her over before we went home. Plus, she had to stop by the house and pick up a few things. She called your phone, but you didn't answer. So, she called Mon and he told her that you didn't stop by the house to get anything last night and she was determined to bring it over here to make sure you were straight. So, don't bring your hog head cheese ass in here hollering at her like you are out of your fuckin' mind," Sia fumed. She put me in my place and walked over to the stove to turn whatever she was cooking off.

"I'm sorry, baby. I just don't want anything else to happen to you." India moved around slowly. I know that was because she was still hurting from what she'd gone through. She hadn't even had time to fully heal from delivering the babies before her body had to deal with yet another trauma.

"It's okay. Just know that no matter what I'm going through, I'm always going to make sure my family is good. You'd do the same for me," she told me and kissed me on the cheek. I wasn't having that though. That kiss on the cheek is for friends and we were far more than friends. I pulled her in to me and passionately kissed her. I made sure that it was as gentle as possible. She flinched up a little, so I pulled away from her.

"What are we eating?" I asked. That was my way of finding something to talk about before she had a chance to go off on me from stopping the kiss we were engaged in.

"I'm doing smothered pork chops, rice and gravy, cabbage, squash/zucchini, homemade cornbread, and a peach cobbler," Sia announced.

"Why are you cooking all of that for breakfast?" I quizzed.

"Breakfast? You don't know what time it's?" India probed.

"No. What time is it?"

"It's after two o'clock in the evening. You didn't make it back to the house until around three o'clock this morning. We could've woken you up, but you needed the sleep," India beamed. I was thankful that she was looking out for me, but there was really no time for me to sleep when our babies were still out there doing who knows what with who knows who.

"Mon, you ready to get out of here?" I queried.

"As soon as I fill my stomach up, then we can do whatever you want to do," he told me. All of a sudden, I heard a loud commotion coming from outside. I went and looked out their bay window and saw every member of the crew there.

"What's going on?" I asked them.

"You saved my friend's life and I know y'all are about to go out there and embark in more dangerous situations to bring my Godbabies home, so this is a way that I can repay y'all. Making sure you're well rested and have a full stomach." Sia smiled.

"She's got a point," Mon insisted. There was really nothing I could say behind that other than, "thank you".

We all sat down in their formal dining area which was big as hell to eat. Chucky even had a woman on his arm. It was the Natalie chick that worked with Sia and India.

"When did this happen?" I asked, being nosey as usual. I wouldn't even consider it being nosey. We were a close-knit family so it was a must that we knew everyone that stepped inside of our circle.

"We been fuckin' for a minute now. I met her when Sia and Mon got shot. She was in the room checkin' on Mon when I got there," Chucky told us.

"Checking on Mon for what? We never work that floor," Sia stated. She stood from her seat with her hands on her hips. Mon dropped his head. "Did you fuck her?" Sia asked.

"Come on, Sia. This not the time for that," India spoke.

"Shittin' me. When it comes to my man, there's always a time for this shit. You know just like I do that if she said something suspect about Zelle, you'd beat that ass first and ask the questions later," Sia suggested.

"Yeah, you're right, but not after the night we had."

"If Mon would just answer the question then you wouldn't have to worry about me going off."

"Sit down, ma. Why you think I gotta fuck everybody?"

"Because I know about the python you working with. It don't take shit else for the next bitch to find out about it because your ass stay trying to wear shit that shows your print. Not to mention, you know hoes be talking." Sia was going on and on about Mon's dick. His ass sat there laughing with the other men around the table. My mind was somewhere else, so I didn't care to indulge in their laughter.

"Sit down, Sia. I didn't fuck with ol' girl. That's all Chucky," Mon finally informed her.

"I know the fuck it is and it better stay that way. You better not hurt Chucky either. He's like a brother to me and India and we will drop a hoe behind him." Something told me that Sia and India didn't really care for Natalie that much. We were going to have to get details as to why a little later.

The rest of the meal went off without a hitch. I tried my best to relax a little. People were laughing and sharing memories. We even talked about some crazy shit that happened when we first started this street shit. I must admit that those were good times. We fucked up a lot along the way, but I felt like we'd matured enough to know not to make those same mistakes. At least that's what I always told myself until we ended up in situations like this or other bad as situations.

No matter how much I tried to clear my mind of the bad thoughts I was having, I couldn't. There was no way for me to have happy thoughts with my seeds on my mind all the time. Something needed to happen to get them back home and I meant soon, or more bodies were about to start dropping.

Chapter Eighteen:

R'Mondo

As we sat around talking, my focused stayed on Zelle. He didn't hide the fact that something was on his mind. I knew it was about the triplets and there was no way that anyone can blame him for that. No matter how hard everyone tried to help him ease some of his tension, nothing that we tried worked. When we'd finished eating, Sia and India came in with some desert. It was homemade apple pie, my favorite.

We sat there until everyone had their food and something to drink. It wasn't an alcoholic beverage in sight because we needed to keep our mind clear.

Ting... Ting... Ting...

That was the sound of Zelle hitting the wine glass that sat on the table in front of him. That nigga stood up like he was about to give a speech. Every eye in the room was on him as we all got quiet.

"I know y'all are doing this to help me and India keep our mind off what's been happening and that's cool. But I can't lie and say my babies aren't on my mind heavily. With everyone here, we need to do a quick rundown of all the old shit this nigga has done and the shit we found out recently. It's time we map this shit out for real because I swear I'm about to be on a war path and y'all know what it's like."

"He's right. We need to lay all this shit on the table. Did everyone bring what they were supposed to bring?" I asked, standing from my seat as well.

"Yeah, we got you," Chucky stated. He stood as well.

"Ladies, y'all stay in here. Men, y'all meet me in the living room." As soon as all the men stood from the table, India, Sia, and a few of the other women stood as well.

"What the fuck are y'all doing?" Zelle roared.

"These are my babies too."

"And my Godbabies."

"Yeah," the other women said in unison.

"We are all about to be updated on what happened and what needs to happen to get them home safely. If you have a problem with that, then oh damn well. If you continue to try to leave me out, then you better know that I'm going to go behind your back and try to handle this shit myself," India insinuated. The other women agreed with her. The only person that didn't say anything was Natalie.

"Get your ass up, bitch! We in this shit together," Sia's mother told Natalie. I damn near fell out laughing. They weren't cutting her ass any slack. It made me wonder if she'd done something to India and Sia that we didn't know about.

Sia came over to me and whispered in my ear, "She fucked Yo-Yo." My brows raised although I tried my best to maintain the same composure. "She doesn't think I know, so don't say anything."

"After the way y'all are treating her, I'm pretty sure her ass knows something," I whispered back to her. "Now, bring your fine ass on in here. The sooner we get the babies back, the sooner I can get off in that," I informed her. I discreetly grabbed her pussy. It was fat as fuck. I started to tell Zelle that I'd be back, but I couldn't do my boy like that.

We convened in the living room. I had Chucky go to my office and grab the whiteboard. I hung it up on the wall.

"I know the fuck you did not?" Sia fussed.

"Calm down, baby. You act like we not about to move anyways." We'd found a house that was close to India and Zelle's house, but the house was too out in the open for me. Not only that, but the homeowners' associated had too many stipulations for this neighborhood. I was in the process of having a house built for us that she didn't know anything about. Zelle was doing the same for India. In fact, both of the houses were right next to each other and were going to be inside the same steel gate where we'd have somebody sitting at the entrance for security 24/7. This shit with the kidnapping put a lot of things in perspective for us. Zelle and I were going to do whatever we could to keep our families safe from this day forward. Sia and India knew that we were going to move, but Zelle and I kept the details about the move to ourselves. We were going to keep it that way until the houses were finish and we were able to take them there to surprise them.

"Chucky, go ahead and give us a rundown of what we already know," I told him. Chucky stood at the board and wrote out what we already knew.

"So, I'm going to give everyone a brief rundown of shit. Link and Cynthia first surfaced to get back at India for some bullshit reason. Link claims that someone paid him to come after Zelle and Mon, but he never mentioned who it was."

"What about the nigga Uncle Rocko came to the last meeting that we had with? Nobody had ever seen him before and nobody knew anything about him," Peanut reminded us.

"That's true. When I asked Uncle Rocko about it, he kept brushing it off saying we'd know in due time," I chimed in.

"Exactly. Not to mention, he has been acting a little strange," Zelle spoke up.

"What do you mean? What have you noticed?" I'd noticed Uncle Rocko acting fucked up ever since he told me about turning things over to me, but I wanted to see if anyone else had noticed some of the things that I noticed.

"You know when you were in the hospital and me and the crew took Tiny out?" Zelle asked.

"Yeah. Why?"

"He rode with me. We saw that the bitch had a bomb on her, and we all took off running. Uncle Rocko didn't. He came out with only a few seconds to spare. When I asked him what took him so long, he said it was because he was old. You know like I do that Uncle Rocko would never refer to himself as being old." Zelle was right. Uncle Rocko was the only man I knew that didn't want to tell anybody how old he really was.

"Why are you just now saying something? I could've questioned his ass about it."

"Question him for what? You know he was going to lie. That nigga don't care about nothing. He on some sneaky type shit."

"Well, we could've at least had someone following his ass."

"You know that wouldn't have worked either. He is too smart for someone to follow him and he not know it. He's been in these streets for a while. You really can't put shit past him," Zelle acknowledged. I had to admit that he was right. Uncle Rocko was smart as fuck. There was probably nothing we could do that we'd be able to get over on him with.

"Let's get back to the situation at hand. Uncle Rocko has nothing to do with the babies coming up missing so we are going to have to worry about him later," Chucky asserted.

Now, that was true, but I made sure to put a note on the whiteboard that said: Check in with Uncle Rocko. That was so I'd know that I needed to look a little closer into what he had going on. Something was definitely off about him and I was going to do whatever I needed to do to find out what it was.

"As of now, Link is dead. Tiny is dead. Cynthia is the only one who's still kicking, but that won't be for long. Link is gone so she's unprotected. It won't take much of shit to get to her," I told everyone. "Now, Chucky has an additional list of addresses that Link frequently visited. Cynthia has to be at one of those addresses. We have to find her and find her soon. The way I figured it, we can all split up and go to these addresses. Three people to a car. We are bound to find her somewhere. Whomever finds her needs to hit the rest of us up and stay with her until we can all get there. We also have to be very cautious on how we go in. There are babies involved," I continued.

"I want to be there before you kill her. I want to ask her why? Surely, the reason she gave me up has to be something more than what she told me. Nobody would put that much energy into killing or hurting someone over the little poor as excuse that she gave me." I agreed with India. There certainly had to be something more to what both Cynthia and Link had to say about the reason India was given up. When we questioned Link about it, he made it a point to say that Cynthia was the only one who could give us the answers we were looking for.

"I'll let you come in to question her, but I won't let you be around when she takes her last breath. That is your mother and you'd forever have nightmares behind that. I love you too much to have to see you suffer with those nightmares," Zelle told her. I didn't blame him. That's one of the reasons Zelle didn't allow Sia to be present when he got rid of Tiny.

"Fine," she stated. She pouted a bit, but nobody cared. Her little ass was lucky she was told that she could come in to question her because if it were up to me, Cynthia's ass would be dead the minute we got the babies out of her grasp.

"Mon, it'll be you, me and Chucky," Zelle instructed.

"Why the hell Chucky always get to come with y'all? You make it seem like he's more important than we are or some shit," Junebug said. Everyone in the room looked at him like he was out of his mind.

"Because Chucky has been with us since day 1. We all know each other's movements," Zelle explained. That was something I wouldn't have done. We were in charge and therefore, whatever we said was how it was going to be. All that other bullshit was irrelevant as fuck.

"Don't explain shit to him. Matter fact don't even worry about going Junebug. We'll catch you later," I told him.

"What? Now, y'all not about to be fuckin' with my coins. We all know that when we get to go out on missions like this, we get paid good as fuck because we are putting our lives in danger. Why would you tell me not to go out?"

"Because at the end of the day, your ass don't know who the fuck is in charge. If you took your ass to McDonalds and them niggas told you to make a fuckin' Big Mac, you gonna make that shit with no problems. Even though you not punching a fuckin' time clock, Zelle and I are the fuckin' management team. You don't have the right to question us. However, since you felt the desire to, that clearly shows that you aren't worthy to work up under us. Today was your last day part of the team. We'll hit your ass up with a severance package later," I told his ass and pointed for the door. He stood up like he was about to run up on me and all the other niggas in the room stood. Even Sia got out of her chair.

"Fuck you think this is? If you touch my man, you won't touch no fuckin' body else," Sia quickly threatened his ass. My baby was a ride or die no matter what. Even though she didn't have to stand up for me, she did and that meant a lot. Most women would probably crumble at a time like this, but not Sia.

"It's cool. That nigga not gonna do shit. Hit the road and I'm not saying that shit again." That was the last warning his ass was going to get before his body was sent home to his mother in pieces. Junebug had been with us a while and had never stepped out of line like that before. For some reason, strange shit had been happening with all of our *Day Ones*. At that point, I really didn't know who I could trust.

Chapter Nineteen:

Chucky

Finally, a nigga got a chance to speak. Everyone in the crew had been jealous of me for a while. It had nothing to do with me per say, but everything to do with the amount of money that I made. Zelle and Mon paid me good, that's why I opted out of having a family. The shit we did was dangerous, and I didn't want to be in the same situation that Zelle had found himself in. Both his girl and kids were taken. That's a tough pill to swallow. It would especially be bad if he was never able to find them or they were killed because someone was out to get him. Yeah, they could have that family shit. It wasn't for me.

Junebug had been making a lot of smart-ass comments that I let slide. The fact that he was bold enough to say the shit in front of Zelle and Mon said a lot. He clearly didn't value his life. Had we been anywhere other than where we were, they would've killed his ass for even acting like he wanted to ask a question. Junebug wasn't a fool. He knew that within a matter of a few hours, his ass would be dead. He knew too much about the organization and he moved like he was against us. That only meant that he was going to be a causality in an issue that he caused amongst himself.

"Everybody jealous of my man," Natalie boasted. She came up to me and wrapped her arms around my waist. I removed her arms from around me. "What's wrong?" she queried.

"Now ain't the time for you to be boasting about me being your man. We both know this is just a fuck thing."

"If it was only just a fuck thing, why the fuck you bring me here with everyone else that's important in your life? They had their wives, fiancé's and girlfriends with them."

"Because you are the only one I'm fuckin' with at the moment. Trust me, if there was someone else, I'd bring them instead of your thirsty ass."

"Wow, why are you talking to me so harshly?"

"I didn't like the way you embarrassed me," I told her. She looked confused. "When all the women stood up to ride for their nigga, you sat your ass there and didn't move."

"You just said you weren't my nigga, so why should I stand up for a nigga that wasn't mine?"

"You don't get it, so don't worry about it. Come on so I can take you home. I'll hit you up when I'm free."

"You don't have to take me no damn where. I'm more than capable of getting home on my own," she sassed. She was furious at me and I could understand why. Still, she needed to see things from my point of view. If I even thought about making her my woman, the fact that I knew now that she wasn't going to ride for me showed me that she was not for me. Not with the business I was in. It's sad to say, but it was very true.

Natalie stormed out the house and went outside. She could've at least stayed her ass inside to wait on the damn Uber or whomever she called to pick her up.

"I'm going to wait outside with her crazy ass. I'll be right back," I told everyone else.

"Uh huh... You going to make sure her ass not mad at you. I don't blame you. The woman holding that good pussy is never the one to piss off," Mon teased. "You can go out there and join her. I have Link's phone and his finger to unlock it. We'll be lookin' into this shit until you get back from doing that Keith Sweat beggin' and shit," he continued to joke. I smirked and opened the door to go out behind her.

RATATATATATA... RATATATATATAT... RATATATATAT...

Gunshots erupted the moment I stepped outside. I surveyed the area and couldn't spot Natalie anywhere.

"Shut the damn door." I heard someone yell. By the time I tried to close the door, it was too late. I'd taken every bullet that was sent towards my body. The difference between Mon and Zelle being shot was that they were able to make it out of the shit alone. There was no coming back for me. I'd taken one too many bullets to several of my vital organs. That was it for me. My eyes shut and my body wavered as I took my last breath. It was then that my body hit the ground.

Chapter Twenty:

Sianni

"Sia, where the fuck are you?" Mon called out for me as he and the rest of their crew made their way to the front door. They were returning fire to the fools that decided to shoot my house up. Even my father had his gun out, shooting back. "SIAAAAAA..." Mon called again.

"I'm right here," I finally answered him.

"Get behind me," he commanded, and I crawled towards him. India managed to make it to where Zelle was and when I searched for my mother, I saw her near my father.

"Who is shooting at us?" I asked Mon, but he ignored me. I knew it wasn't a good time for me to ask him that, but I was scared. I'm sure not as scared as India was when she was kidnapped, but I was pregnant. I wanted to live to see my baby being born and to marry Mon. Hell, I haven't even been to my first doctor's appointment yet.

Mon turned and looked at me. He placed his hands on the sides of my face. He glanced into my eyes.

"You already know what I need you to do, right?" I shook my head. He wanted me to get all the women and try to get them to one of the back bedrooms.

"Ladies, stay low, but follow me," I screamed. The shoots were still ringing out.

"I'm hit," someone yelled. I turned around just to make sure it wasn't Mon. For some reason, I couldn't see him. The men had all gone outside the house to shoot back. My nerves were all over the place, but I had to do what Mon asked me to. That was the only way he'd trust that I'd know what to do in the event that something happened.

We got to the bedroom all the way in the back corner of the house. Everyone stayed low. I crawled towards the closet to see how many of us would be able to get inside of it if we needed to. That was because Mon had the closets fixed to lock from the inside. I'd planned to stick a few women in there and take the rest to the room across the hall from it. When I opened the closet, the first thing I noticed were Yosef's clothes. I knew he'd taken his shit and left, so how the fuck did his clothes get in here and how the hell didn't we see the shit when Mon was getting the closets fixed? The shit didn't make sense.

"Sis, you must've had a house guest or something," India said to me. I turned to look at her and she was pointing at the bed. It appeared that someone had been sleeping in it. There was no way Yosef had been sneaking in and out the house and we didn't know it. "Sis? Are you okay?" India asked.

"Uh yeah, I'm fine." I wasn't going to tell her anything about what she'd seen until I got with Mon and we figured out what the fuck was going on.

"India! Sia! Ladies!" someone yelled.

"Yeah?" India and I got to the door and cracked it open. Zelle was standing right outside the door.

"We've got to get out of here," he told us.

"Where are we going?" India asked.

"The men are about to take the rest of the ladies home. I'm about to get you and Sia to Sia's parents' house," he remarked.

We rose to our feet and made our way back to the living room since the shooting had stopped. We stepped outside and there were bodies everywhere. Mon was kneeled over a body that he'd thrown a white sheet over. I already knew who it belonged to.

"I'm sorry, Mon." I placed my hand on his shoulder in an attempt to comfort him.

"I'm going to kill Cynthia's ass. She's the one behind this, but we need to know who's helping her. That bitch couldn't have done this shit on her own."

"I know, baby. But right now, we need to call the police and get out of here."

'Y'all go ahead and leave. I'll call the police as soon as I know everyone is safely away from here." Whether Mon knew it or not, I was not about to leave him. The shit with Chucky was something that was going to fuck all of us up. It was no doubt in my mind who was behind the shit. Mon and Zelle think it's Cynthia. I don't. Nobody did that shit but Junebug. He was jealous of Chucky and looked for the perfect opportunity to take him out and this was it.

With the men focused on bringing the babies home, they were not on high alert that someone else would come after them. This left them vulnerable and open for Chucky and whomever else Junebug saw as a threat to be killed.

By the time everyone had left, the police had come speeding up to our home. Mon and I stood out there talking to the police and giving them as much information as we could without telling on ourselves and the other people that were inside the house. They didn't need to know that we had a party, and someone was kicked out the crew. They surely didn't need to know about the babies missing. We both knew that getting the cops involved would make things bad for us and we wouldn't be able to move the way we wanted to without worrying about if the cops were watching or not. However, we had no choice because the shit happened outside. Our neighbors were nosey and probably called the police as soon as the shouting started.

Mon was quiet after speaking to the police. He went inside the house and sat on the couch. He had poured himself a glass of Hennessey and Coke. It seemed like he wanted to be alone, but I couldn't find it in my heart to leave him. I needed him to know that he was not the only one hurting behind this. Losing Chucky was a hard ass pill to swallow.

"Baby?" I called out to him.

"What Sia? Why are you still here?" he yelled at me.

"Why are you taking your anger out on me? I'm only trying to be here for you."

"I don't need you here. I need you to go be with your parents like I said. We can't be together right now. Being with me is only putting you in more and more danger," he exclaimed.

"Mon, don't make me hurt you. I'm not about to go anywhere. No matter how far you try to push me away. You can say whatever you want, but I'm not fuckin' leaving." He stood from where he'd been sitting on the couch. He threw the glass of liquor that was in his hand against the wall and stepped in my face.

"Oh, hell naw," my father grunted. He started walking towards where Mon and I were standing, but I threw my hand up to stop him. Mon would never lay a hand on me because he loved and respected me too much. He was only acting out of anger from being hurt about what happened to Chucky. This was going to be the one and only time that I allowed him to step to me on some bullshit.

"I got his, dad. Give me a few," I requested.

"I'm not leaving you in here with his ass. If he touches you, I'll have to kill him," my father threatened. I knew he meant business. But at the same time, I also knew that Mon wasn't the type to back down from anybody. No matter who it was.

"Mom, please take him out of here. Mon isn't going to touch me," I assured them. My mother was a little hesitant, but she finally pulled my father out of the living room behind her. They went inside the kitchen because it was close to the living room and they could get to me if they needed to.

"Mon, baby, I know this is hard for you and I'm sorry. As much as I hate to say this, I really don't believe Cynthia was behind this. Think about what happened during the meeting. Junebug got mad and y'all put him out. He'd been gone long enough to set up a drive by. Besides, the way he stood up and spoke about Chucky always being with you and Zelle spoke volumes. That meant it was an issue that he always had on his mind and he was waiting for the best time to say something about it," I explained.

Mon stared into my eyes. He never said a word. I knew that was his way of taking in what I said to him.

"That makes sense, but I'm tired, Sia. I'm tired of all the bad shit going on around me. Do you know I'd die if something happened to you? That's how much I love you and my seed that's growing inside of you." For the first time, I saw tears slide down Mon's face. Yeah, thugs had soft spots too. I was sure that was a side that he only showed to me. That led me to believe that he really did love me as much as he told me that he did.

Pulling Mon into me, I embraced him as if that would be the last time I'd ever see him. I wanted to comfort him any way that I could. Although he was taller than me, he was able to lie his head on my shoulder. My shirt felt wet from the tears that were freely flowing from his eyes.

"Marry me..." Maybe I had hallucinated and heard something that I wanted to hear after hearing those words.

"Did you say something?" I asked him to be sure I wasn't trippin'.

Mon pulled away from me and looked into my eyes. He was still very emotional. He dropped down to his knees and put his ear to my stomach. That was the first time he'd ever done that much to acknowledge the fact that we were about to be parents. He would say little things about the baby here and there, but never had he been so close to my stomach. A few moments passed and he looked up at me.

"Marry me, Sia. I know we haven't been together long, but I also know that I love you. You're the first woman that has ever given me the type of emotions that I have and I don't know what to think. You complete me and give me the feeling of family that I've always wanted and needed. I promise you that once all of this shit is done and over with, I'm walking away from this street shit because it'll never be worth losing you. This shit with Chucky really has me fucked up. I keep losing people that I love and I don't want you to be one of those people. Marry me and let's make this shit forever." Like a baby, I stood before him crying. My mother and father stood in the doorway of the kitchen with their eyes glued on us. My mother was crying more than I was. My father started a slow clap before they finally stepped inside the living room to join us.

"Answer him, girl. You better marry that man," my mother said in between tears.

"Yes... Yes... YESSSSSSSS..." I started jumping up and down. It didn't matter that he didn't have a ring or that it wasn't in front of a lot of people. The people who really mattered most in my life were present, minus India. I was sure she wouldn't mind. Love was love and the way I felt about Mon was something I didn't want to lose either.

Mon finally stood up and pulled me in for one of the tightest hugs he'd ever given me. I didn't know what I'd done to deserve the man God sent me, but I would forever be grateful for him.

"You sure you want to marry me?" he asked.

"Yes. Why would I not be sure?" I replied.

"Cool. Let's go get married then," he told me.

"Say what nih?"

"Why does it have to be this big extravagant wedding? Why can't we get married with the people who matter the most to us being there? I want to do this today," he stated. There was not a look of uncertainty anywhere on his face. He really wanted to get married today. I was speechless for the first time in a long time.

"Well, what are you going to do, girl? We got money to make this shit happen today and you know it," my father reminded me.

"Yasssss bitccchhhh... You better marry that man," India screamed. I turned around to find her and Zelle standing behind me.

"What the... How the..." There were so many questions that I wanted to ask that I couldn't even get out of my mouth. "When the hell did you come back?"

"We never left. Mon had planned this already, but the shooting fucked it up. It may not be the most appropriate time for him to ask that considering everything that has gone on and is continuing to go on, but we needed some happiness in our lives. You think I was going to leave out that door without watching my bestest bitch get proposed to?" India ranted on and on.

"When did he even have time to plan a proposal or get a ring or anything?" I asked India when I should've been asking Mon.

"I didn't. I told them that today was the day that I wanted to ask you to marry me because it was my mother's birthday. She's not here, but I wanted something to happen on this day that would make me happy instead of always feeling sorrow because she is no longer here. It was right before India came up missing that I talked to her and Zelle about this and they thought it would be a good idea. I was supposed to have a ring and this big elaborate proposal planned, but when India and the babies came up missing, I dropped everything. I decided that I was going to just wait before I did anything. Then the shit that just happened to Chucky and all this other bad shit happeneing around us has been draining for me. I need some happiness in my life and making you my wife is the happiest thing that could ever happen to me," he explained.

It was a lot for me to take in, but I completely understood where he was coming from. It was clear that he wanted to get married today, but that I couldn't agree to. I wanted our Godbabies to be a part of my big day. So, until they were back home safe and sound, going forward with getting married was not something that was about to happen.

"I love you, Mon. I really do, but I can't be selfish right now. Our Godbabies are out there and we don't know where. I want them to be a part of our big day so I can't marry you until you go handle that."

"Her ass just scared that you might not come back home," Zelle cracked. I shot him the side-eye because that was also a part of the reason I didn't want to rush getting married. I didn't want to get married today and be a damn widow tomorrow.

"I completely understand, but as long as you said yeah, we all good. We'll handle the logistics and shit once the babies are home. Right now, Zelle and I are going to pay Chucky's family a visit to let them know what happened. Y'all need to go ahead and go home with your parents," Mon instructed.

"When are you coming back home?"

"Let's not worry about that. Zelle and I have shit to do. I'll check in with you when I can."

Mon saying that to me gave me an unsettling feeling. I already knew that meant he was going to be out of pocket for a while. It wasn't that I was scared that he was going to be doing something he had no business doing, but I knew that he wasn't going to sleep until they got the babies back home.

"Okay. Be careful. I love you." There was so much more that I wanted to say to him, but I couldn't. Too much had happened for me to think about putting up a fight.

Zelle and India bid their farewells while I was loving on Mon. It was sad for both of us to watch our men walk out the door not knowing if they were going to return to us. We knew they had a job to do. It was a bittersweet moment, but India and I did what we were told. We got some stuff from the house and left with my parents. For some reason, I felt like this was going to be the last time that I'd see my house.

Chapter Twenty-One:

Zelle

(Two Days Later...)

It had been two days since the last time Mon, and I had laid eyes on India and Sia. It wasn't because we didn't want to, but because we've been busting our assed in the streets trying to track down Cynthia and Junebug.

We've had limited sleep and haven't really slowed down to enjoy a decent meal. Today was the day that we were finally going in on Cynthia's ass. We tracked her down to one of the houses that we least expected Link or her to be at. It was crazy that she was still roaming around like nothing had happened. A few of our men spotted her and had been stuck to her ass, following her every move. They said that each time she moved, she had two other women with her. The two other women appeared to be walking around in disguises. They had on a different wig, head scarf, hat, and even different sunglasses whenever they stepped out so it was hard for anyone to decipher who they were. They brought pictures to us and we couldn't positively identify them. However, Mon kept saying that there was something familiar about them to him. He could never put his finger on what it was.

"What are you going to do about India?" Mon asked me, removing me from my thoughts.

"I'm going to let her little ass show up to say whatever she needs to say to the bitch but then she has to go. I'd never let her stick around and watch me kill her," I replied.

"I feel ya. I bet she's going to try to bring Sia's ass along with her."

"You know she will, but that's cool. She won't be around for it either. However, she can help India get the babies to the hospital. They are going to need a full and thorough examination after this bullshit."

There was a moment of silence between us. I thought back to when Mon proposed to Sia. That meant that India was going to be pressing for me to propose to her. It wasn't that I didn't want to, but I felt like there were still some things we needed to work through. Yeah, she seemed to have forgiven me for what happened between Pixie and I, but I really believe she's only acting that way because of the recent events that have occurred. First, she was caught going on a date with another nigga. Even though the date didn't happen, that was her intention and I wasn't sure I could get passed that. Then the kidnapping shit. It was all too much. The love we had was real, but I wasn't about to marry her because I loved her. Marriage was something that was meant to be forever and if I felt like we were at that point, then I would have no problem putting a ring on it.

"Why'd you ask her to marry you?" I asked Mon. I was very curious as to how he thought Sia was the one and they hadn't been together long at all.

"What do you mean? I love her."

"I know you love her, but you haven't been together long. How do you know she's the one?"

"I can remember when I was younger, my father used to always tell me that you'd know when you found the one. He would say how he could never imagine his life without my mother and how she made him a better man. Yeah, Sia and I haven't been together long, but I know that I love her. Each time she struggled with picking me over Yosef hurt more and more. When she finally made the right choice, I told myself and God that I would spend the rest of my life making her happy. We've been through more shit in the little time that we've been together than most couples will go through their entire life. Sia's it for me. She completes me. I can tell that I'm leaning towards being a better man. She even has me ready to give up the street shit and you know we used to always say that we were going to the grave being hustlers. That shit changed the minute I met her. She's carrying my seed. There ain't no way my baby is coming in this world without their parents being in the same household and without us having the same last name. However, that's just me. Each person is different," he expressed.

"I love the hell out of India and the month I spent without her was hard as hell. The shit she did with trying to move on like I didn't exist bothered me and like I said, the fact that her ass had talked to that nigga about what we had going on was something that didn't sit well with me. She didn't know him. She didn't know if his ass was out to get us or not. Yet, she felt comfortable enough to tell him whatever she told him about us."

"How long are you going to hold that against her? You felt comfortable enough to slide your dick into another bitch. If she can forgive you for that then you shouldn't have a problem with forgiving her for what she did," Mon told me. It made sense, but it was easier said than done.

"You may be right, but you know our mind don't work like that. Look how you acted when Yosef sent you that video of him fuckin' Sia on the balcony."

"Don't remind me. I wanted to kill that nigga then. Sia just don't know it, but the minute his punk ass pops back up, it's over for him. I'm going to make sure his ass don't ever bother her again."

"My point exactly. You had fucked other bitches and didn't find anything wrong with it because y'all weren't in a relationship. She was in a relationship with Yosef when she had sex with him, and you were ready to cut the nigga's head off."

"Yeah, well that's different," his ass chuckled.

"No, it's really not. The shit hurts men more than it hurts women when they do some shady shit to us. We can do some fucked up bullshit everyday and the minute they find out, we want them to forgive us. When the shoe is on the other foot, we be ready to fuck some shit up. We aren't as forgiving as they are." That was the truth.

"You'll get it together. I know you and India are meant to be. Don't allow your mind to talk you out of what you deserve and that's happiness. I know y'all have gone through some shit, but what's a relationship without trials and tribulations? That's how you learn to communicate, trust, and lean on each other. A person that tells you they have a perfect relationship is a whole fuckin' lie. Nobody gets it right but as long as you can push through together, it'll work out in the end." That made a lot of sense as well.

Mon was right when he said that Sia had changed him. In the short time that they'd been together, I've seen a whole new man. There's nothing like loving someone and having them love you in the same manner. It was something that India and I shared at one point, but it seemed like we may have lost each other along the way.

My phone started beeping when I was about to say something else to Mon. I picked it up and it was a message letting me know that they'd gotten Cynthia. I didn't think to ask if the babies were with her or not. I just knew I needed to get to her as soon as possible. I shot Sia's father a text and told him to bring India to the meeting spot. I told him about it when I told him that I was going to allow India to question her bitch as mother. That's where I told our guy to bring her mother too. This shit was ending today.

"You ready for this?" I asked Mon as he pulled away from the house we'd been watching to see if her or the girls that we were told had been with her would show up. We literally had been sitting in front of the house for a whole day and never saw any sign of her.

"I'm as ready as I'll ever be. If I don't get back to Sia soon, she'll probably put out an APB. You see how she keeps blowing my phone up. Don't let me miss one of her calls, her ass starts going off like I'm purposely dodging her."

"You sure you're ready to marry her and deal with that for the rest of your life?"

"Hell, yeah. That's my queen. I'll never not want to be with her. Stop overthinking shit because you're beginning to doubt your relationship and that's never good."

"Have you heard from your Uncle Rocko or heard anything about Yosef or Junebug?"

"I know where Yosef's ass is. I just haven't touched him yet because I'm trying to give him the opportunity to apologize to Sia for all the pain he's caused her. He knows I'm waiting for it because I sent a message to his ass. If he doesn't, then both of his parents are going to come up missing. Simple as that."

"You don't think it's crazy how he just packed his shit and left without saying a word?"

"He did say a word, he just didn't say it to Sia," Mon chuckled.

"What the hell did you do?" I laughed.

"I may have given him a little money and told him to leave. I was the one who moved that nigga's clothes. I've been hiding them in one of the guest rooms in the back of the house," he admitted.

"You cold blooded for that. I hope it wasn't in the room you told Sia to take the women into when those fools were shooting outside," I asserted.

"Damn. I didn't think of that. Sia hadn't said anything so hopefully she missed it." Mon stopped talking. It seemed like he was thinking about something. Then, he suddenly said, "As far as Junebug's ass goes, I know where he is too. However, we both know he's going to show up at a Chucky's funeral to try to take the suspicion off him.

That's when we are going to grab his ass. Uncle Rocko is someone I haven't heard from in a minute. I'm not sure what's up with him, but that will be addressed as soon as this ordeal with Cynthia is done and over with. I can promise you that. Family or not, if he crossed me, he will suffer the consequences." He was changing the subject and I allowed it. There were certain things that people didn't like to talk about, so I understood the need to discuss something else.

"You know I got your back," I assured him and I meant every word of it.

"Oh, fa sho. I'll never question your loyalty," he told me. He dapped me up as we pulled away from the house we were at. We headed straight to our meeting spot. It was time that Cynthia was handled. I was also going to see if the housekeeper I used to fuck with was working so I could get her ass too. I didn't forget how she allowed someone to pay her to come in on our meeting and I had a real feeling she had something to do with Link getting to our money. It was a matter of time before she took her last breath and today was going to be that day.

Chapter Twenty-Two:

Cynthia

It was tiresome as hell trying to take care of three babies and keep myself safe in the process. I had two people working with me to help, but we had to be careful because all of us didn't need to be caught together. If we were, then we'd all be killed and everything that we'd done would have been in vain. That couldn't happen.

"Are you okay?"

"Yeah, I'm fine. I'm just tired of all this running. Maybe we need to take the babies and leave town," I suggested.

"Now, why the fuck would we do that? I'm not allowing India to have a happily ever after. She deserves to die for the pain she's caused in our lives." I was reminded.

"You're right. I gotta keep my mind clear. The more I worry, the more I'm setting myself up to be caught."

"Well, maybe your ass worried too much because your ass is caught," a man's voice spoke. I turned to run but realized I was surrounded. There was nowhere for me to go. The men grabbed me and the women that were with me and led us out the house.

They took us to a hotel. I kept thinking they were going to rape us. That was until I thought back to what Link had told me about the meetings Mon and Zelle liked to have at a hotel. It was obvious that we were being taken to them. That meant that Link was already dead, and it was now our turn to pay the piper.

When we got inside the hotel room, it was crowded. The one person there that I wasn't expecting to see was India. Did they bring her there to kill me? I laughed on the inside because I knew she'd never have the heart to kill her own mother.

"India," I greeted her. I even stretched my arms out to receive her for a hug.

"Kill the bullshit, Cynthia. You know good and damn well we aren't on friendly terms so you can miss me with the bullshit," India told me.

"I was just speaking. You obviously brought me here to talk, so at least let's be cordial with one another."

Smack...

"Don't fuckin' stand there and try to patronize me." India slapped the shit out of me without warning. My reflexes had my hand go up in the air and before you knew it...

Smack...

I'd smacked her ass back. India charged at me and started wildly swinging. I dropped down to the floor hoping to trip her, but that didn't work. She kicked me in the stomach, causing me to roll on the floor in pain. She then got on top of me and sent blow after blow to my head. After a while, she picked my head up and started banging it against the floor. The entire time she was doing it, she was cussing me out. She called me everything but a Child of God.

"Get her off me," I yelled but nobody came to my rescue for at least another ten minutes.

"Come on, baby. Let's ask her what you want to know and then get out of here. We've given her way too much energy," Zelle told India. He pulled her off me and sat her in a chair. There was an empty chair placed in front of hers. That's where one of the guys sat me so I'd be facing her.

Suddenly, the door to the room flew open and in walked the two women that had been working with me.

"Adrienne? Tiny? What the fuck! I thought you said she was dead," Mon roared.

"Tiny was in the house with a bomb tied to her. I don't know how the fuck she's standing before us," Zelle exclaimed.

Tiny stood there with a smirk on her face. Mon walked up to her and that smirk quickly vanished. The expression on his face showed that he meant business. If Tiny didn't start telling him what he wanted to hear, he was going to kill her ass before she could blink.

"How are you here?" Mon asked her.

"When everyone ran out of the house, someone stayed back to help me get lose. They thought I died in the house, but I didn't," Tiny explained.

"Uncle Rocko!" Zelle stated. "Remember when I told you how he took his time coming out the house and he said that it was because he was old? The whole time, his ass was in there letting this bitch free. But why?" Zelle questioned.

"That's because he knew I didn't deserve to die. There's a lot about your uncle that you don't know. Besides, why would I leave this world and leave my aunt to deal with you demons alone?" she commented.

"What you say?" Mon stepped a little closer to her.

"You heard what I sa-"

Pow...

Tiny never had a chance. Mon shot her in the forehead before she could finish her statement. He didn't care what she had to say about his uncle or what part she played in what Link and I had in store for India.

"Your turn," Mon told Adrienne as he stood in front of her. She was so scared that she pissed on herself. "Don't get scared now. You obviously weren't scared when you agreed to work with my enemy," he told her.

"I'm sorry. I never meant for things to go as far as they did. I told Cynthia that I would help because India cost me so much."

"What the fuck did I do to you? I don't even know you?"

"You're my sister. My father was married to my mother when he started messing with Cynthia. Cynthia was very young. My father told her to abort the pregnancy and she didn't. She tried her best to force herself into his life. That's when it came out that he slept with a minor. His life was ruined. He was fired from his job. My mother no longer wanted anything to do with him. He was shunned by the whole community. That made him commit suicide."

"What the fuck does that have to do with me? I was a child. I was innocent through all of this. I didn't ask to come into this world. I didn't ask our father to be Chester the Molester," India cried. "My mother gave me away for a man that didn't want anything but her pussy. She was a young hoe and that had nothing to do with me. Then she ended up giving me away and keeping Link. What the fuck sense did that make?" I stood there listening to Adrienne and India go back and forth. Adrienne turned her attention on me because India made a lot of sense. Adrienne was so damn dumb. She never expected to be caught in a situation where she'd lose her life. She opened her mouth to say something to me, but I didn't want to hear it and apparently, neither did Mon.

Pow...

Mon shot her in the back of the head. Blood splattered on me. That freaked me out. I was never a person that liked blood.

"You want to start talking now?" India asked me.

"No. I have nothing to say to you. You ruined my life. Had you never been born, my life would be so different," I assured her.

Waaaahhhhh.... Waaaahhhhh....

The sound of babies crying resonated throughout the room as two of the men came walking into the room carrying the triplets. India took off running to the babies. So did Zelle and Sia.

Clap... Clap... Clap...

I began to clap at how dramatic they were being. They weren't that damn happy to see the babies. India came over to me and...

Smack...

She slapped me once more. The way Zelle stood behind her, I knew not to hit her ass back. There had to be a way I could talk my way out of the situation I was in. How was India going to stand there and allow her boyfriend to kill her mother? How could she even stomach being in the room when it happened?

"Handle her, baby," she told Zelle before passionately kissing him. "Let's go, Sia," she said. Sia, Sia's mother, and India took the babies out the room.

"Please India, don't leave me here with them. They're going to kill me," I cried for India to come help me. She turned around and waltzed back towards me. I just knew she had softened up and was going to do what she could to save me.

"Bitch, I don't care if he tied your ass to the back of a car and drug you down the street. See, you've done nothing but make my life a living hell. You had Tiny set my man up with that Pixie bitch so they could fuck, and you could send me the video on a day that was supposed to be special to me. You tried at every turn to ruin my life. And for what? Because you were jealous of me. This had nothing to do with you being mad that my father took his life. It had everything to do with the fact that you gave me up thinking I wasn't going to amount to shit. You kept Link because you figured he could take over the streets when he was of the right age. You sent him to my nigga and his friend thinking they would take his ass under their wing and when they didn't, you were out to get me because you were pissed that I had everything you always wanted. But guess what bitch, you'll never have the life that I have. You could never walk a day in my stilettos. So, go ahead and take this bullet like the bad bitch you wanted to be," India spat. I watched as she rolled her tongue around in her mouth and spit on me. "Scum ass bitch," she muttered and then walked away.

The look on Zelle and Mon's face showed that they'd had enough of what I'd done to them. There was nothing left for me to say. I closed my eyes and started praying that God would forgive me from all the things I'd done wrong. If I would've known that my life was going to turn out the way that it did, I wouldn't have fucked with India or her man in the manner that I had.

In the midst of me praying, India stopped walking. She turned to look at me once again.

"I want to know one more thing," she said.

"What?" I said with a lot of attitude.

"Where the fuck did you keep Link all this time? How is it that you were fine giving me away and not him?" She had tears in her eyes.

"Link stayed with my aunt. She couldn't have kids and she'd always wanted a son, so she took him. Nobody wanted your ugly ass. I tried to keep you until I realized I didn't want you either," I admitted.

"Yeah, go ahead and end this jealous bitch's life," she spat and continued on out the door.

India was right about one thing. I was jealous of her. She had the life I always wished that I had. A man that loved me and would walk through fire for me. Not having to want for anything, being smart, having a family to call my own, and most importantly, having a support system that would be there for me through thick and thin. That was something I never had and because of all the shit I did, something I'd never have.

Greed took over. Instead of me trying to have a relationship with India, I tried to get rid of her. I would've been better off trying to build a relationship with her and having her take care of me then going against her. I'd fucked up and now it was too late. I opened my eyes long enough to witness Zelle push his gun to the temple of my head.

"Tell Link we said what's up?" Zelle said.

Pow...

Just like that, it was over for me.

Chapter Twenty-Three:

India

If it were anyone else, they'd probably feel some type of way about their boyfriend killing their mother, but I didn't. She deserved everything that happened to her for the turmoil she caused in my life. She gave me up and I was okay with that. She left a note painting this perfect picture of her in my mind when everything that she had me thinking was a lie. Why come back for me when you never wanted me in the first place?

As soon as my babies were back in my arms, I could've broken down crying. I thanked God so many times from the time they were given to me to the time we made it to the hospital. I was grateful when the doctor came back and told me that they were perfectly fine.

The doctor did say he was going to keep them overnight to run a few more tests. He was a doctor that we knew personally and therefore I was comfortable telling him what happened. It made sense for me to do it even though it was something that we were supposed to keep within the family. In my opinion, it was better safe than sorry.

"What the doctor say?" Zelle finally stepped inside the room. I ran over to him and hugged him. The tears wouldn't stop falling from my eyes. In the midst of me hugging him, I realized that he was hugging me the same way he used to. There was a time when it seemed as though the love he had for me was fading. While my thoughts should've been on the babies and the fact that they were safely home, I couldn't help but to wonder what was going to happen with my relationship.

"They are keeping them overnight to monitor them and run a few tests to make sure they are okay. So far, everything has come back good," I explained to him.

"That's good to hear. You must've told them what happened," he insinuated.

"I only told Dr. Peters because we knew him. He told me that he would keep this between us but felt compelled to keep the babies overnight just to make sure everything was good. I thought it was best that he knew so that he'd be able to do a full workup on them."

"I understand." Zelle walked over to where the babies were in the cribs. A smile appeared on his face. That was the first time I'd seen him smile in a while.

"Can we talk?" I asked him.

"Now, is not the time," he replied.

"Now, is the time. I need to know where we stand. Please, just hear me out," I pleaded with him.

Knock... Knock...

"It's open," I yelled.

Sia and Mon came walking inside the room. They both looked exhausted, but I could tell they were happy to see that the babies were okay.

"Hey boo, how are you?" Sia greeted me.

"I'm okay. Ready to be at home." I meant that because I was tired too. I wanted a nice hot shower, something good to eat, and my bed.

"I know, girl. I'm just happy that you and the babies are okay," she told me.

"Me too." Zelle and Mon stood over in the corner engaged in a conversation. It almost seemed heated. I silently prayed that they weren't about to tell Sia and I that they had to hit the streets again. I just wanted all this shit to be over so we could move on and put it behind us.

Especially, Zelle and I. I loved that man with every part of me and I was not going to allow him to walk out of my life.

"Why you looking at them like that?" Sia asked me. Instead of answering her, I shrugged my shoulders. I was in such deep thought on what I needed to do. Apologizing to Zelle wasn't working out in my favor. He needed to know that he's the one that I love. I could admit when I fucked up and when I did something that was wrong. If he would've done it to me, I would've tried to kill him and probably never would've forgiven him. He needed to understand that I understood how he was feeling.

"I need everyone to sit down," I rubbed my temple and started pacing back and forth. Beads of sweat formed on my forehead and my palms had gotten sweaty. Nervousness had taken over me.

"Are you okay, sis?" Sia asked me. I threw a finger up to tell her to give me a minute.

"Please sit down," I requested again. They kept their eyes on me the entire time. Not once did my pacing stop. I was gathering my thoughts. It took them a minute, but they finally took a seat.

Turning to face them, I felt like I was going to pass out. Maybe things would've been easier for me if I'd asked Sia and Mon to leave out of the room. Zelle would probably scorn me later, telling me that the conversation was something that we should've had in private, but I just couldn't. I needed Mon and Sia there for emotional support. Plus, I felt that if push came to shove, I'd have them around to take my side. Don't get me wrong, they'd check me if I were in the wrong, but this time, I think they'd see things my way.

"Sis?"

"Look..." I twisted my fingers. Not once did I stop to look anyone in the face or stand still. It was the best way I could think of to handle my nerves.

"What is this about?" Zelle quizzed.

"I want to tell all of you that I'm sorry. Everything that has been going on lately has been because of me. I know you're probably going to tell me that it wasn't my fault because I couldn't control what Link and Cynthia did, but I still felt the need to apologize." I paused for a few minutes.

The whole room was quiet. That was getting the best of me. I wasn't looking for them to say anything because I had the floor, but a cough or something would've helped me out a lot.

"What I'm trying to say is, thank you. You've been there for me at times when I didn't want you there or when I'd given up on myself. That says a lot. Most people don't have that love and support and I really can't think you enough for everything you've done for me."

Pausing again, I took my time going over to where Zelle was. His eyes were watery, but he never allowed a single tear to drop. Me on the other hand, had a shitload of tears cascading down to my shirt. I got down on my knees between Zelle's legs and grabbed ahold of his hand.

"Baby, I fucked up when I went out on that date. You think I was looking for someone to replace you, but I can assure you that I wasn't. I just wanted you to see what you had and know that whenever you do me wrong or get to a place where you no longer want to be the man I needed you to be, there was always someone else out there willing to do so. Nobody was ever going to get near this pussy. Your pussy. Nobody certainly would ever get close to my heart because you have it and have had it since the first day I laid eyes on you. You think I told this man about our relationship and I promise you that wasn't the case at all. We had a conversation about why we were single, and I told him that I was tired of men lying, cheating, and stomping over my heart. That's something I'd tell a random stranger if they were to ask me that. He just twisted my words to lead you to believe that I was really talking to him about you. Never in a million years would I discuss you with the next man nor will I ever allow him to talk down on you.

"You may not want to believe that, but that's the honest to God truth. You hurt me and I wanted you to hurt more than me, so I did what I did. There's no coming back from that and I understand that. But you have to think about the way I felt when I saw you fuckin' that Pixie bitch. You were all into it with your eyes closed and shit. That's the shit you do with me."

"But diid I fuck her the way that I fuck you?" Zelle interrupted me.

"What?"

"You heard me. Did I fuck her the way that I fuck you? Did I kiss her all in the mouth, caress her body, or even show that I cared enough to make her nut?"

"No, bu-"

"But hell. There is no buts. I know I fucked up. It was something to do because we'd been together for so long and I'd only been with you. Sometimes I get scared that we won't make it because you like to argue about stupid shit and I'm not here for that. I love you, but I get tired too, India. I want the same amount of respect as you want. I trust and love you and I want you to give that to me. You get so complacent at times with our relationship that you stop doing the shit that you used to do in the beginning. I've been that way at times too, but we can't do that. We have to keep the same motivation we had from the jump if we're going to make this shit work. I know you were mad at me, but that didn't give you the right to leave the house that we shared and take the babies away from me." Him sitting there telling me what rights I had was about to anger me. How the fuck could he sit there and tell me what I had the right to do after he'd taken my heart out of my chest and stomped on it?

"No matter what, we're going to continue to disagree on what happened. At the end of the day, I love and want only you. I want my family. I want us to be together forever and you have to want that to."

My talking ceased. I was giving him the chance to say something else, but he didn't. It almost made me feel like he was trying to make me feel worse than I already felt, but I was done talking. I was going to say one last thing and be done with the conversation.

"I love you. I can't say it enough. I want to spend the rest of my life with you. When I thought you'd died, I didn't know how I was going to carry on. But you came back to me. I don't ever want us to be apart. Will you marry me, Zelle?"

Most women would say I was out of my damn mind to ask this man to marry me, but why? I loved him and I felt he loved me too. Why should a woman feel bad for proposing to a man that she wanted to spend the rest of her life with? I wasn't ashamed of any of it. If I had to ask him in front of an entire arena of people, then I would do it.

"No," he replied.

"Excuse me. Come again..." I wanted him to repeat what he said to make sure I heard him correctly. Did this nigga really tell me that he wasn't going to marry me?

Zelle stood from his chair and moved around me. He stood at the babies' cribs for a moment and then headed for the door.

"Don't ever ask me to marry you again," he stated. There was a look of disappointment in his eyes.

"What do you mean no?" I asked. I still wanted to be sure I wasn't trippin'. Mon and Sia sat there not saying anything. They had to be in just as much shock as I was. There was no way this shit was happening. His ass turned down my proposal. It made me feel like I made a damn fool out of myself.

"NO, I WILL NOT MARRY YOU," he roared. Fear took over me and I jumped.

"Why?" My tears started to fall faster. How could he be so damn insensitive. Was he about to walk away from our relationship? From our family?

"Because I said I'm not. Your little ass thinks that you have to do tit for tat in every situation. Who wants to spend their life in a relationship like that? I told you from jump there would be times that I fucked up. Well, that was the one and only time that I actually did. Don't think I don't know about the time you were texting one of your classmates because you claimed I wasn't giving you the attention that you claimed you deserved. You emotionally cheated and I physically cheated. Cheating is cheating. Remember that there is no one sin greater than the other," he reminded me. So, not only did he tell me he wasn't going to marry me, but he also wanted to quote the bible. What kind of fuck shit was that?

"I told you I was wrong. I'm not going to spend the rest of our relationship doing that. I know that our relationship is strong and that we can get through this shit. If I would've thought that you'd want to walk away from me after going on an innocent date to make you jealous, then I never would've done it," I admitted.

"That's the thing. You didn't think. You were pissed off and allowed yourself to do something that there was no coming back from, but I'm not going to take the shit. If you felt that I wasn't doing something right, then you should've told me. If you felt like our relationship was failing, then you should've told me."

"And if your punk ass thought that you couldn't be with one woman for the rest of your life, you should've told me. Hell, I know how to role play. I'd buy wigs, different toys, dress like a hoe, and do whatever else I needed to do to keep the excitement in our sex life where you wouldn't have to go to the next bitch."

"This isn't about sex, India. It's about keeping the lines of communication open. There's nothing wrong with you or our sex life. I fell weak and did something stupid as fuck. I'll regret that for the rest of my life and will spend the rest of my life trying to make the shit up to you." Well, at least he did say he'd spend his life trying to make it up to me. Did that mean he wasn't breaking up with me?

"What are you saying?" I had to be sure. Nothing would make me feel better than to hear him actually tell me that he wasn't walking away from what we had.

"I'm saying that I'm sorry. I never meant to hurt you or our family. I'm not gonna lie and say that I wasn't fucked up behind what happened with you and ol' dude, but I know I caused it on myself. I had a long talk with Mon while we were lookin' for the babies about love and how he knew Sia was the one for him. Everything that he said to me made a lot of sense."

"What the hell did he say?" I glanced back at Mon and Sia who were sitting there holding hands.

"He just made me realize that my life would be nothing without you. And the reason I told you no to your proposal was because I'd never accept a proposal from you. I'm not saying that it's wrong for a woman to do, but you're my queen. The last thing you need to be worried about is getting down on your knees for me; unless you're giving me head." I punched him in the arm for playing with me. "What? I'm just saying," he chuckled. Then out of nowhere, Zelle got down on one knee. He grabbed ahold of my hand and glared into my eyes.

"India, you're the only one that could ever make me feel love. You've created a man in me that I'd never thought I could be. You've given me the greatest gifts I could ever ask for on this earth and you made my house a home. I don't want to even think about being away from you or my family. Will you do me the honor of being my wife?" he asked me. It was as if a dam had broke because more tears feely flowed from my eyes. I could feel snot sliding from my nose. I was doing one of the ugliest cries I'd ever done.

"Yes baby. Yes, I'll marry you," I told Zelle. He stood up and spun me around. Sia ran over to me and gave me a big ass hug. So, did Mon.

It was crazy how shit took a turn for the better once all the negativity had been erased from our lives. While we were standing there happy, there was still a problem lurking in the shadows. There was still the issue with Yosef and Uncle Rocko. How they were going to handle it, I didn't know. What I did know was that nothing was ever going to come between my family again.

Chapter Twenty-Four:

R'Mondo

Both Sia and India being engaged at the same time was going to be a headache. If I would've known that Zelle was going to propose to India, I would've held off on my proposal. That was simply because if we went to their house or they came to our house, all we would be forced to talk about would be the wedding. What had Zelle and I gotten ourselves into?

Zelle pulled me to the side while the women were talking. I already knew what he was about to talk to me about; the issue with Uncle Rocko. It was hard for me to believe that Uncle Rocko would do some conniving shit, but then again, you really couldn't trust anyone. My father used to tell me that there was no loyalty in these streets. I wouldn't think he'd mean that the people closest to us would be the one's we'd have to watch out for.

"You good, man?" Zelle asked me while Sia and India continued to talk.

"This shit is crazy. Why would Uncle Rocko let Tiny go? What does he have against me? The shit not adding up."

"I know, but you know I got your back. I'd never let shit happen to you."

"I know that, but I think this is something that I'm going to have to handle on my own. It doesn't make sense at all. At the same time, I don't want to just go off what Adrienne and Tiny said. I need answers and the only way to get the answers I want and need is to get face-to-face with Uncle Rocko."

"Yeah, and I understand you want to handle it on your own because he's the only family you've had for a very long time. Nix that... He's the only biological family you've had. Blood couldn't make us any closer," Zelle corrected himself and he was right. There wasn't a single person alive that could tell me that Zelle wasn't my brother. We've been through so much shit together and have always had each other's back. I'd be a damn fool to think of him as anything but a brother.

"I know you're like family, but when we get there, let me do all the talking," I commented. It wasn't meant to be rude, but it was really something that I was going to have to do on my own.

"I got you. When do you want to do this?"

"The sooner the better. I understand you just got your babies back, so you can chill with them and we can deal with this Uncle Rocko shit at a later time," I suggested.

"Nigga, we ain't had no good sleep, no pussy, or no good meal in days. When I get to the crib, it's a wrap. I'ma sleep, fuck, and eat until I can't no more so you might as well gon' get this shit out the way now," he chided.

"Bet. Let me hit him up and see what's good."

Me: Sup Unk?

UR: Not shit, Phew. Sup wit you?

Me: I need to meet up with you about something. You got time to see me?

UR: I'll hit you up some time next week. I got shit to do this week.

The fact that he wanted to wait a week to see me let me know that something was up for sure. He'd never pushed me off like that. No matter what he had going on, his ass always made time for me. For whatever reason, he was acting funny and I was more than ready to get to the bottom of it.

"Why you looking like that? What he say?" Zelle questioned me.

"He said some shit about meeting up next week," I replied.

"Next week? Since when did his ass start pushing you off like that? Yeah, something's not right and we need to find out what it is ASAP," Zelle told me.

He was right. There was no way I was going to wait another week to get to the bottom of the bullshit. I needed answers and I needed them now. Whether he wanted to give them to me or not, I was going to get them. I especially wanted to find out what was up with him bringing the mystery man to one of our meetings. He knew just like everyone else that we never had outsiders come to our meetings. Not the meetings with our crew and that was for good reasoning too. We didn't need them to know what we were up to and we certainly didn't need them to familiarize themselves with the crew. If that happened, then when we needed to put someone in undercover to find out some shit for us, we wouldn't have anybody to use because the stranger would know exactly who it was. Unk was moving around lookin' foul and shady at the same damn time.

Me and Zelle walked over to the ladies. They stopped talking and just looked at us.

"You're leaving again, aren't you?" Sia asked me.

"Yeah, but I swear it's the last time. After this, I'm leaving this shit alone," I assured her.

"Do you promise?"

"Yes. I promise," I told her and kissed her on the forehead.

"Don't even ask me because I done already told your baldheaded ass that I wanted to marry you. That means I'll be back," Zelle said to India because she could say anything to him. He rolled his eyes and acted like he had an attitude. The shit was funny as fuck.

"You make me so sick," she said and kissed him. We hugged our ladies and left out the room. We told them that we'd be back, but truth be told, we never knew what was going to happen in the street world.

Zelle hit up the crew to let them know what was up. He told them where to meet us at. Even though I didn't know if what Tiny said was true or not, I knew that I had to be prepared for anything. Uncle Rocko wanted me to show up next week, but I couldn't jig with that. He was about to have to tell me something or else he'd have to lose his life.

Chapter Twenty-Five:

Uncle Rocko

So what if I'd had my own little issues with Mon? He was going to find out what they were in due time. It wasn't his fault that I had a problem with him, but he was still going to have to suffer the consequences. That was the code of the streets and he knew that shit.

He hit me up talking about he needed to talk, but I wasn't in the mood for the shit. Being at home, minding my business, was the only thing I cared to do at this point. Business was going well, and life was good for me. He wasn't about to ruin my night with whatever bullshit he had going on today.

"You ready for me, daddy?" Tara came in and asked me. She was naked as hell and I was loving the view. I liked to call her Star because she was bright as fuck. I'd met her one night that I was hanging out with Link and had been fuckin' her ever since.

"Bring that fine ass on in here so I can put this dick in your life." I may have been old, but I was far from dead. Besides, apparently Tara liked the way I made her body feel or she wouldn't keep coming back for more.

"Mmmm... Let me taste that dick, baby," she directed, and I obliged her ass. I laid in the bed on my back with my dick at full attention. She got in the bed with me on her knees and popped my dick in her mouth like it was a blow pop.

"Yeaahhhh... Suck that dick. Gag on that big mufucka."

Truth be told, my dick was only about seven inches, but because I wasn't circumcised, it added to how thick my dick was. The thickness of it drove bitches crazy. Then the fact that I could fuck was a plus. So, when these hoes be hollering size matters, let them know Uncle Rocko said they a whole lie.

Pumping up, I pushed my dick as far in Tara's mouth as it could go. She started gagging on it. The slob coming from the corners of her mouth turned me on even more. I placed my hand on the back of her head and continued to push my dick in her mouth. Tears were running from her eyes and snot was coming from her nose. That still didn't make me stop. I was punishing her ass for that smart ass mouth she had.

"Take this shit. You know you like it when I'm rough with you. Don't ya?"

Smack... Smack...

"You like this nasty shit. Huh slut?" I always talked to her like I'd just picked her up off the side of the road. That was a part of role playing that we did quite often. I smacked her in the face a few more times leaving a red handprint on her cheek. "Get up there and ride this big ass dick," I ordered.

Happily, Tara got on top of me. It took her a while to push me all the way inside of her because of the thickness, but when I was in, she wasted no time bouncing up and down on my dick. The shit felt good as fuck. I started moaning like a bitch.

"Mmmmm... Yeah baby. Give me that dick. Fuck this pretty pink pussy," she instructed me. I started pumping faster inside of her. The faster I pumped, the faster she bounced. I felt my nut rising, but I wasn't ready to nut yet.

"Slow down," I requested, but she ignored me.

"Naw. You don't want me to slow down. You supposed to be beating this pussy up, nigga," she chided. Tara placed her hands on my chest and began slow grinding on my dick.

"Damn Unk. You gettin' it in. Check him out, Zelle." The sound of Mon's voice made me sit straight up. I pushed Tara off me so roughly that she flew on the floor.

"What the fu-" Tara opened her mouth to say.

Pow...

"Shut up, bitch!" Tara never had a chance. Zelle shot her between the eyes right as she was about to speak.

"What the fuck you do that for?" I queried, using my feet to push my body up to the head of the bed.

"Keep moving and I'll go ahead and kill you," Mon stated. The look in his eyes told me not to chance it with him.

"What are you doing here? Didn't I tell you that I would meet with you next week? What is this shit?"

"This shit is me coming to find out what your issue is with me? Why did you let Tiny go knowing she tried to kill me and my girl? Why the fuck would you team up with Cynthia and Link to try to take me and Zelle out? What did we do to you other than love you? You were like a father to me."

"Oh, cry me a fuckin' river. You sound just like your damn weak as father right before I ended his life."

"What did you just say?"

"You heard what I said. Don't be a pussy. Man the fuck up! That was the one thing I never understood about him and you mother. He was weak and where he was weak, I was strong. I looked better, went further in life, and had more money than your father. Yet, she still chose him over me," I confessed. Mon used his gun to scratch his head. I knew he was confused about what I'd just said to him, but I was more than prepared to clear up the confusion. If it was my time to die, then it was just my time.

"You were fuckin' my mother? You betrayed your own brother?"

"Let's be clear, he was my half-brother. I met your mother first. I kept spitting game at her, but she kept shooting me down. Then, your father went in trying to talk to her. I guess she liked the nerdy kind because she started throwing the pussy at him. Then she got pregnant by him. He hurried up and married her because he didn't want a bastard child. Too bad you ended up being a bastard anyways," I chuckled.

Pow...

Mon let off a shot that barely missed my head. I reached under my pillow to retrieve the gun I kept under there. That was one thing I always taught Mon. Always keep protection nearby, no matter where you are. That's how Tiny knew to remove the gun he had under his pillow when she went in to kill him and Sia. Someone thought in advance because the gun wasn't there.

"Oh, Tara didn't tell you that she got a call to remove all of your guns? Damn! Looks like you're shit out of luck," Zelle informed me.

"If she was working for y'all, then why'd you kill her?"

"No witnesses. That was another thing you taught us," Zelle stated. Mon stood before me speechless. I jumped out the bed because if I was going to die, I was going out like the real man that I was.

"You know, it's crazy how much I looked up to you and all this time, you're the reason that my parents never got the chance to see me become the man that I've become."

"Don't forget how you became that man. If it weren't for me, you would've been in the system. You wouldn't have all the street smarts or money that you have now. You should be thanking me. That's something that your father never would've taught you."

"You think this street shit is what made me? You're fuckin' wrong. I'm far beyond this shit. Then you came to me actin' like you loved me, and you cared. Why even say something to me about taking over for you if you didn't mean it?"

"Oh, so now you got your little girlfriend and she having that little baby of yours, you think you're a better man than me? Your mother was my world. I loved her from the moment I laid eyes on her, but your father took her from me."

"How could he take something you never had? My mother wanted no parts of this street shit. God sent her the man she was supposed to be with, and it wasn't you," he barked. "My mother was too good for you. She had dreams and aspirations. The same thing my father had and if it weren't for you, they would've been able to do everything they ever dreamed of doing." He pointed his gun at me. I wasn't the least bit worried because he was getting teary eyed and his hand was trembling. There was no way he'd be able to shoot me. I meant too much to him.

"Well, unfortunately nephew, they had to die and while you're standing here arguing with me, you need to be mindful of the man that's coming for your girl," I announced.

"How much longer do we have to continue to do this bullshit? I think he's pissed off that Alfonso has decided he no longer wanted to work with his ass," Zelle finally spoke. I glanced over at him to see what all he knew.

"What?" Mon probed.

"When you were in the hospital, I did a little research. Turns out Uncle Rocko hadn't been fulfilling all the promises he'd been making to Alfonso and he was being asked to step down. Alfonso was looking at you taking the reins. Rocko's ass just came to you with it first, so once Alfonso said something to you, you'd think it was a suggestion from Rocko. Now, I see that this nigga really trying to take you out because with you out of the way, then Alfonso would have to keep putting up with Rocko's bullshit," Zelle explained.

"Is this true?" Mon asked me like I was really going to answer his ass.

"Maybe it is and maybe it's not," I answered.

"What about the man that came to the meeting with you?"

"That was one of Alfonso's men. He came in to see how you and Zelle handled business so he'd know if you would be good to take over for me. The fact that you allowed me to walk on in with him showed that you were off your game. Both of you are too fuckin' trusting. Why do you think all this bullshit keeps happening to you?" I remarked.

"Fuck it," Zelle bellowed.

Pow... Pow... Pow... Pow... Pow... Pow...

Zelle started emptying the clip on my ass. My body jerked left and right a few times before hitting the ground. I didn't die immediately. Mon came over and kneeled down beside me.

"For a long time, I only dreamed that I'd become the man that you were. At least, who I thought you were. Now that I know the real you, I see how much of my father was really inside of me. Had you come to me on some grown man shit, I would've told you to keep this shit because I don't want it. Anything that can take me away from my family or make me fuck over those that's been loyal to me ain't worth having. I hope you rot in hell."

Pow....

Chapter Twenty-Six:

Sianni

(Two Weeks Later...)

To say that things were back to normal, would be a lie. Mon and I had finally gone to the doctor, Dr. Karen of course, and found out that I was three months pregnant. To be exact, 15 weeks and 4 days. That was great to me considering all of the shit that we'd gone through. The stress from the events alone was enough to make me lose the baby, but God saw fit for me to keep it. That was a blessing in disguise.

"You ready for this?" my mother asked. India and I had still been staying with my parents.

Mon and Zelle came back and told us what went down between them and Uncle Rocko. It saddened me to see the hurt in Mon's eyes when he was talking about it. Who would've thought that the man he looked up to would've been his enemy? That makes you wonder who you can really trust.

The men spent three nights with us at my parents' house before they went back out into the streets. They said it was because they had to tie up loose ends, whatever that meant. India tried to explain it to me, but I still couldn't grasp what she meant. The streets aren't for me and it was going to remain that way.

"Hellooooo... Sianni, what are you thinking about?" my mother probed, to get my attention. I'd been gawking at myself in the mirror. While I was wearing all black, I still looked fat and I hated it.

"I'm sorry, mom. I was just thinking about the shit that's gone on these past few months. It's crazy how my life has taken a whole 360."

"Yeah, it is crazy. But, that's life for you. You can't determine what'll happen, but you can determine how you're going to handle whatever happens." Those were facts. Life was only what we made of it, right?

"You're right. I just don't think I'm ready for this. If you would've told me years ago that I would have to go with my fiancé to bury one of his closest friends, you couldn't have paid me enough to believe it. Chucky didn't deserve to die," I expressed.

"You're right, he didn't, but Mon needs you, so you're going to have to be strong for him through all of this," she refuted.

"I know and I plan on doing so. I just hope he doesn't shut down on me. I can remember plenty of times when dad would be going through some things and he'd shut down on you because he didn't want to involve you in his mess."

"Honey, your father didn't shut down on me. He just made it a point to never discuss certain things in front of you. That was because we wanted to keep you as far away from this mess as we possibly could. Now that you have a man of the streets, you understand more of the life I had to live when you were younger."

"Yeah, I do, and I don't see how you do it. Being away from him for days and worrying if he's going to come back to me scares the hell out of me."

"I know the feeling. At least you know he's walking away from the business. I'm glad about that because I can rest knowing that nobody is going to come after you or my grandbabies," my mother joked, rubbing my protruding belly.

"Grandbabies? What you talkin' bout, Willis?" I said to her in my Gary Coleman voice.

"You are going to give me more than one, aren't you?"

"Mon claims he wants six, but he'll be lucky if he gets two out of me. I loved being an only child, but it got lonely. That's why I said he'll be lucky to get two. The changes a baby puts your body through is not something I look forward to at all. Then I crave some of the weirdest things. I hope I don't end up like those people that eat the Argo Starch and Clay." I cringed at the thought of it. People eat some of the craziest shit. I saw one woman on TV the other day talking about how she ate tissue. Fuck kinda shit was that?

"Yeah. I know that's right. That's why I only stopped at one. Look at your momma in her forties and can pass for your sister," she teased and started doing a small twerk. My mother could be off the chain sometimes, but that was why I loved her.

"Yasssss.... What y'all got going on in here?" India stepped inside the room and started popping my mother on the butt. That only made her try to twerk a little faster and harder. All I could do was shake my head.

"If you don't sit your old ass down somewhere," my father roared as he stepped inside the room.

"Whatever. Don't come in here acting like you don't like what you see. Later on, you'll be trying to get me to do it on your dick," my mother announced.

"Shidddd... Why we gotta wait 'til later?" my dad refuted and licked his lips.

"I think I'm going to be sick," I stated and grabbed ahold of my stomach while putting my other hand in front of my mouth like I was puking. They started laughing but I was so serious. Who wanted to think about their parents having sex? That was a visual that I could live the rest of my life without seeing.

"Whatever. Come on, we need to get this show on the road," my father muttered. He was upset about Chucky's death too. He did his best to hide it, but we all knew that he and Chucky had formed a bond since we'd been around Mon.

My parents drove India and I to the funeral. The triplets stayed with India's parents. They were young and wouldn't understand death, so India didn't think a funeral was the place for them to be and I agreed with her wholeheartedly.

By the time we made it to the church, Mon and Zelle were rolling up in the family car with Chucky's mother and siblings. His mother was a mess. Chucky took care of her and his siblings. He'd been doing so since he was 14. They depended on him for everything. That's why he was so big on family and treated us as such. That was one man whose loyalty never had to be questioned.

India and I got out and joined Mon and Zelle with the rest of Chucky's family. The whole crew was there, and everyone knew to be dressed in all black. If you wore anything but that, you were subject to get ejected from the church. Black was Chucky's favorite color and Mon and Zelle were going to make sure everyone honored that.

When it was time to view the body one last time, I stood by Mon and held his hand, but not one time did I look down at Chucky. I couldn't stand to see him in that manner. The crazy thing about it was that Junebug's ass had skipped town and no one had heard from him since. However, Mon and Zelle had people on the lookout for his ass. They even put a bounty on the nigga's head for one million dollars. The streets definitely talked then. No matter where Junebug went, his ass would never be safe.

Chucky's mother got up to the casket wearing one of her mother of the church hats. It was all black and had a black crow on the top of it mixed with some funny looking flowers. I didn't know who allowed her to leave the house like that, but they needed their ass beat for doing so. She wailed out like someone was killing her when she saw Chucky. That was her oldest child and only son. He was also her only source of income. She didn't work and wasn't trying to because like I said before, they depended on Chucky for everything. So, I wasn't sure if she was crying because he was dead or because she knew her ass might really have to get up and do some hard labor.

The funeral lasted well over two hours. When they opened the floor for people to give those three minutes of expression, so many people walked up to speak on Chucky's behalf. He even had a few hoes pop up, which was even funnier. Natalie didn't dare take her crazy ass up there and I couldn't say that I blamed her. It wasn't until Zelle and Mon went up there that I could no longer contain my tears.

Chapter Twenty-Seven:

Zelle

For people like Mon and I, you'd think it would be easy for us to talk in front of a large crowd. We were really introverts, but because of our positions, nobody ever knew that. The church was packed, and I swear half those people, I'd never seen before. People were all in the balcony and standing outside the church in honor of Chucky. I could only pray that I had that many people show up for me.

"We've known Chucky for so long that he became more than a friend to us. He was a brother. Most people knew that he worked for us, but he really didn't. Up until the day that he took his very last breath, I always told him he was our right-hand man. He embraced not only us, but our families. He'd go out of the way to do any and everything for anybody." Mon paused. He was getting choked up. I wanted to tell him that was good since we only had three minutes, although other people had taken ten to damn near fifteen minutes to speak. The funeral was set up like Chucky was a celebrity. I guess when you looked at it, he was a celebrity to the people who knew him.   He was loved and liked by everybody,except Junebug's punk ass.

"You can talk," Mon told me, passing me the mic. I wanted to hit his ass in the back of the head with it because we both agreed that he'd do all the talking. Because Chucky was a part of our organization, it was only right that we spoke up for him. But damn, I wasn't the one trying to speak.

"Look, Chucky was a nigga from the streets. Rough around the edges like most of us are. He didn't take shit from nobody. I remember when we were younger. This big nigga named Whiskey came up on him talking shit. Now, we called the nigga Whiskey because he always smelled like pee. Of course, by the way Whiskey was in the bottle, it look just like pee, but we knew the teachers wouldn't let us get away with calling him Pissy. So, Whiskey it was. Anywho, Chucky was a lil' small mufucka back then. He's what you'd call a small dog with a big ass bite.   Chucky didn't fuck with nobody and he dared anybody to fuck with him. Well, Whiskey was the dummy that tried Chucky. Man, he tried to Debo Chucky one day and Chucky body slammed the fuck out of his ass. It was like a midget beating up a sumo wrestler." I laughed. Everyone else in the church was laughing too.

"You do know we in a church," Mon whispered to me.

"And? Them niggas cuss too," I replied. "Ever since that day, nobody messed with Chucky. Mon and I told him that we needed him around to be our bodyguard. We were joking at the time, but whoever knew it would really happen. We trusted him with our life, and he lost his trying to protect the ones he loved. He gotta be smiling down at all the people here showing their love for him. I'll never forget that nigga." I glimpsed down at the casket. "You my nigga for life," I stated. That's when a lone teardrop fell from my eyes. I meant every word of what I said.

"To Chucky," Mon yelled, holding a blunt in the air. I busted out laughing. This nigga was giving a toast with a blunt. The crazy part was that it was other niggas in the church holding up a blunt too. Now, it would've been some shit if the preacher would've held one up too.

We took our seats and waited patiently for the remainder of the service to be over. We rode to the cemetery to pay our last respects. His mother, of course, did a lot of jumping up and down, hollering, and crying. I wanted to go up to her and kick her ass into the ground with him, but I let her make it.

"Y'all ready to go?" India and Sia came over to join us.

"Y'all gon' back to the church with the family. We gotta handle something," I stated.

"Not today, Zelle. Please!" India pleaded with me.

"Baby, I just have to tie up one more lose end and we'll be good to go," I assured her.

"Promise?"

"I promise, baby. By the time your hungry ass get your food and have a seat, I'll be right there with you," I told her. She couldn't do anything but laugh because she knew I was speaking the truth. India ass was always eating something.

We sat around and waited on everyone to leave the cemetery. That's when we walked over to the shed where the groundkeeper kept all of his supplies. Inside the shed was Junebug's ass. We got a call late last night that his dumb ass came to town because he heard his baby momma went into labor. Isn't it funny how people turn on you?

Yeah, his baby momma was indeed pregnant. Junebug used to talk about the shit all the time, but he fucked up when he shot at Chucky because that would've meant he'd miss the birth of his daughter trying to hide. Well, we went and paid his baby momma that one-million-dollar ransom that we had on his ass and she called and told him she was in labor. That nigga flew back into town in the middle of the night and we had somebody at the hospital waiting for his ass. We had him tied in the groundkeeper's shed so he would know what he caused.

"Junebug... Junebug... Junebug... It's a shame that we have to meet under these circumstances. Isn't it crazy how you went from having everything to nothing at all in a matter of days?" I taunted him.

"Chucky was one of those niggas that you just didn't fuck with. Not only did you shoot and kill him, but you shot inside of a house that all of our women were inside of. How do you think we should handle this?" Mon asked him like he was really giving that nigga options.

"I didn't do it. It wasn't me," Junebug lied.

"If it wasn't you, then who could it have been? We've gotten rid of all of our enemies. You were there, so you know that. You talked all that shit about Chucky like you weren't eatin' good as well. Jealousy is such a fucked-up thing. Now, you get to go to your grave a bitter man," I told him.

Pow... Pow...

That was the sound of me putting two bullets in the back of his head. There was no need to prolong the inevitable. Peanut was there to pick us up. The clean up crew was there as well. We told them to dick a hole and throw Junebug in it, only after cutting his head off and sending it to his mother. At least then, she'd have something to remember his unloyal ass by.

We got in the car with Peanut and had him take us to the hotel we'd been staying in so we could change clothes. There was no way we could show up at the repast with blood on our clothes. There were too many people there and we didn't need them asking questions.

We were ready in a matter of minutes. By the time we got back to the church, there was music playing and people congregating like nothing happened. For once, it felt right being around a big crowd of people. I found India and took a seat next to her. If nothing else came from the shit we'd gone through, I had my woman, my brother, and my babies. What more could I have asked for?

Chapter Twenty-Eight:

Yosef

There I stood dressed in all black wearing a big ass cowboy hat. It was the best disguise I could come up with at the last minute. When I heard about Chucky's funeral, I knew that Sia would be there and there was bound to be a time she'd be alone. That was when I was going to make my move. I'd been hiding out and being quiet, but I was also lurking in the shadows. There wasn't a thing that she done or went through that I wasn't aware of.

Sia sat around laughing and talking with some of Chucky's family members. Mon and Zelle were nowhere to be found and India was too busy on FaceTime to pay attention to Sia.

Patiently, I sat and waited for her to go somewhere alone. Ten minutes passed and she got up from the table. She told them she'd be back. That was when I followed her. She went to the bathroom and tried to shut the door behind her, but I pushed it on her, causing her to fall back.

"What the fuck are you doing? You better leave before they kill you," Sia whispered. The fact that she was whispering for me to leave instead of yelling for help let me know that she still cared for me.

"What are you doing, Sia? This isn't the kind of people you hang around. You think you a project chick now?"

"I don't have to be from the projects to love Mon. You act like because he was in these streets that he isn't a smart man. He wants more than this street life."

"And you think you're the woman that can give it to him? He's been with plenty of bitches and they have all ended up dead. Who's to say that shit won't happen to you?"

"Leave before I scream, Yo-Yo."

"You're not going to scream because you love me. If you didn't still love me, you would've screamed when I was pushing my way in here on you."

"Get the fuck out of here, Yosef. I'm not playing with you. I'll scream."

"Go ahead and scream. I'm not going to stop you." I pulled out the gun I'd taken from Chucky's casket. It was a gold-plated gun that Mon and Zelle had made for him, that they were going to bury him with. The way I saw it, the nigga was dead, so he didn't need it. I needed it more than him, so I took it. It wasn't like anybody was going to know. Well, at least not until now.

"You stole that from a dead man? What kind of dummy are you?" Sia queried.

"Shut the fuck up, Sia. I love you. You're carrying my seed. I'm not letting Mon or anyone else take what belongs to me."

"If it's money you want, I'll give it to you. But you need to leave. NOW!" she scolded.

"Oh, you're willing to give me money to disappear?"

"Yes. How much will it take for you to leave and never come back?" I noticed her fidgeting, but I didn't pay attention to what she was really doing because I had the advantage. She wasn't stronger than me, so I wasn't worried about her whooping me and getting away from me. She didn't have a gun because she wasn't that type of person, so I wasn't worried about her shooting me.

"Give me ten million dollars and you have to promise not to put me on child support."

"You've got to be dumb as hell. This is not your child," she fussed.

"Sia, you don't know how many times I've put shit in your drink to make you sleep hard as hell. I was fuckin' the shit out of you and you didn't even know it. You remember all those times you'd wake up complaining that your pussy was sore? I know you didn't think that nigga Mon was making you feel that way." I chuckled at the look on her face.

"You raped me?"

"I can't rape a woman that belongs to me."

Sia came charging at me, screaming and swinging. I pointed the gun towards her stomach, and she backed away from me. She was now uncontrollably crying. I didn't give a fuck because there were plenty of nights she made me cry when she told me she didn't want to be with me any longer. Nobody throws away a relationship like the one we had.

"When will you have my money?"

"Tomorrow."

"Good. Now, gon' out there and act all happy and shit and I'll call tomorrow. I don't want no bullshit. If I've been hiding this long, what makes you think I can't go back into hiding? I'll find you and the next time, I'll kill you," I threatened her.

Sia was glowing. The pregnancy made her a little thicker than I remember her being. I got inside of her personal space and started smelling her. She smelled just like *Juicy Couture*. That was my favorite scent on her, and she knew it. Since she had on a dress, it didn't take much for me to snake my hand between her legs and grab ahold of the pussy that would forever be mine. I stuck a finger inside of it and began wiggling it around while kissing on her neck. She stood still. It felt like I was fingering a fuckin' statue and it was pissing me off.

"Moan bitch! You know you like this shit! Remember when I took your virginity? I told you then that this pussy would always be mine and I meant that shit. I don't care how many times you let that nigga inside of you, it'll never be how it is when I am inside of you," I told her. "I'll be back," I grunted and removed my finger. She looked at me like she'd seen a ghost. I placed my finger in my mouth and tasted it. "Mmmm... You still taste just as good as I remember," I taunted her.

Sia had 'fear' written all over her face. I'd never seen her look that way. Why was she scared of me? She was supposed to love me the way that I loved her. Had this nigga really taken her heart away from me?

"Are you scared of me?" I questioned her. She didn't answer. She just stared at me. "Answer me..." I yelled.

Knock... Knock... Knock...

"What?" I hollered to whomever was knocking on the bathroom door.

"I need to use the restroom," an elderly lady stated.

"Fuck! You better be glad someone came," I told her. Gathering myself, I walked over to the door. Glancing back at her, I mouthed the word, "tomorrow" so she'd remember that's when I wanted my money.

Sighing, I opened the door to let the woman in.

Bow...

Something hard hit me in the face. Blood started dripping from my forehead. I felt dizzy and my vision became impaired.

"Are you okay?" Mon's voice was heard loud and clear. "Did he hurt you?"

"He put his finger between my legs. He threatened to kill the kids. He told me that he raped me." Sia's ass was singing like The Temptations.

"She's lying," I lied, spitting out the blood that had dripped inside my mouth.

"No, I'm not. He violated me in the worse way," Sia whined.

"Fuck you, bitch!" I spat at her.

"Leave now," Mon ordered. Sia walked past me and kicked me in the stomach.

"Asshole," she screamed and ran out the bathroom.

"See, we tried our best to give you the chance to leave without looking back, but you just couldn't leave well enough alone. Now, my girl telling me you violated her. I'm not sure what she meant by that, but I can't let you live at this point."

It probably would've been smart for me to say that I'd leave and never look back, but that was not the case. As long as Sia was living and breathing, she was mine. Nobody could pay me enough to believe that the baby she was carrying didn't belong to me. It was mine too. I'd been inside her more than enough times to make sure that it was.

"Do you have any last words?" Mon asked.

"Fuck you!" I remarked. I was expecting him to shoot me, but he didn't.

Mon came towards me and kneed me in the stomach. I went flying down to the floor. He grabbed ahold of my head and leaned it back to where he'd have access to my throat. He pulled out one of the biggest knives I'd ever seen and cut me from one ear to the next.

Chapter Twenty-Nine:

R'Mondo

We'd made it back to the church in enough time to see India frantically standing by the bathroom. We pulled her away and asked her what was wrong. She told me that she saw Sia go towards the bathroom, but she hadn't come back out. That's when Zelle put his ear up to the door and heard that nigga Yosef in there talking to her. The walls were thin so Zelle could hear most of everything that was being said. The only reason we didn't bust in the bathroom was because of where we were. If he were doing something too bad to Sia, she would've screamed so I assumed she was fine.

"You need to change again," Zelle told me. That's when I looked down and saw the blood on my shirt.

"Fuck!" I told him and pulled my shirt off. "Call the crew. Let me go check on Sia."

Sia and India were sitting in the sanctuary when I found them. I asked Sia what happened. She told me everything that happened. I noticed that when she told me about what he said to her about raping her, she dropped her head. I held it back up.

"Don't ever be embarrassed about the shit somebody else did to you. I know you didn't cheat on me. We don't know if he was lying or not, but I am going to ask for a DNA test to know for sure if this is my seed," I advised her.

Don't get me wrong, I wasn't telling her that out of spite, but I wanted to know the truth. If it was my child or not, I wanted to know.

"Are you going to leave me if it's not yours?" she asked me.

"Sia, when I told you that we would be together forever, I meant that shit. Just because the baby isn't mine doesn't mean I'd walk away from you. I know you never cheated on me and you never would. I love you, but we have to know if the baby is mine because we need to know about the medical history. What if something happens and the baby needs blood? If it's not mine, then we may have to reach out to that nigga's family for help. I'm just being reasonable. Do you understand?"

Sia nodded her head and leaned into me. India sat behind her rubbing her back. The relationship they had was similar to the one Zelle and I had. They were sisters more than friends and I was glad that she had someone in her corner the way that I did. That was the best feeling in the damn world.

"Y'all good?" Zelle asked us.

"Yeah. You called the crew?" I asked.

"They on the way. I put an 'Out of Order' sign on the door and locked it. It'll stay like that until the crew does what they need to do," he assured me.

"Are y'all done now?" India asked.

"I'm as done as I'll ever be. Now, let's get out of here so I can dig in that pussy," Zelle called himself whispering, but he was loud as fuck.

"Bruhhhhh... You ain't never lied," I cosigned. "Let's go tell his momma bye and get our women the fuck up out of here. Sia been sliding because she been pregnant, but I'm 'bout to take her to the hospital to get checked and the minute the doctor says she's fine, I'm 'bout to rearrange her insides," I boasted.

"Shut up!" Sia laughed. That was the first laugh she had since she came out the bathroom. I was appreciative of that. I'd do anything to see a smile on her face and I hope she knew that.

"I swear I wish I was in there when that mufucka first showed up. I would've punched that nigga so hard in his chest that his heart would've dropped out his ass." We all sat there laughing.

We stood up to go bid farewell to Chucky's family and Sia stopped me.

"Where the fuck you going like that?"

"Like what?"

"Why you got on a damn muscle shirt?"

"Because I got blood on my other shirt."

"Well, you need to take your ass on out to the car. Ain't no bitch bout to be lookin' at my man."

"That nigga momma old. She don't want me," I argued.

"You a whole lie. Old bitches fuck too. Matter fact, we'll catch they ass at another time. Let's roll." Sia grabbed my hand and led me out the church. Zelle and India were laughing their ass off as they followed behind us.

Sia was crazy as fuck, but I was glad the shit with Yosef didn't change her. She bounced back from whatever he said and/or did to her in that bathroom. I'm sure the bounce back had a lot to do with the fact that India, Zelle, and I were always going to be there to protect her, no matter what. Yeah, she was jealous and crazy, but I was glad I was going to have her ass around for the rest of our lives.

Giving up that street shit wasn't nothing. Yeah, the money was good, but it wasn't worth the constant looking over your shoulder or putting the people that you love in harm's way. If I didn't learn anything else from the shit that I've been through, I've learned that you'll always know the people who'll be there for you when shit gets hard. Everybody ain't for you and even the ones that pretend to be, their true intentions will always shine through when the time is right.

I started as the plug next door, but I'm letting that shit go. With my best friend and girl, that's all I need. I never had the family that I wanted growing up, but I have that family now. There ain't shit I'd do differently in life because if I did, I'd never have the love that I have now.

Epilogue:

(Ten Months Later...)

It was 8:00 in the morning and I was still sleepy. Mon and I took turns getting up to change and feed the baby. Had I known that being a parent was going to be this hard, then I would've run in the opposite direction when it came to sex.

Albeit we were tired, there was no time for sleep. My parents had the baby while Mon and I got ready for one of the biggest days of our lives.

"You ready, baby?" Mon asked me as we got in the car and headed to the venue. My nerves were all over the place. The only thing I could think about was not slipping and falling.

"You're not nervous?"

"Why should I be? We've been waiting for this day for a very long time. Plus, we went through too much shit just to get to this point," Mon replied. He was right.

"I wonder how the baby is doing?" I changed the subject. However, I really did want to know how the baby was doing. He seemed a little fussy earlier. He was only five months and I really didn't like to leave him with other people. Mon said I was crazy and should enjoy any break I could get, but you know how that new mommy thing can be.

"He's fine. My mini me is just fine."

You heard correctly. When the baby was born, we did a blood test like Mon wanted. Turns out, the baby really was Mons. We took it as Yosef just lying to get under my skin about raping me. Although, it still bothered me, I wasn't going to let it ruin my relationship. Besides, he was dead so it wasn't like he could do anything else to me.

For once in my life, I felt like my life was complete. I had the man of my dreams. My little bundle of joy gave me utter and complete happiness. My best friend and my Godbabies brought sunshine to my life. My parents loved me through it all. Oh, and please don't let me forget about Zelle who turned out to be just as much of a brother to me as he had been to Mon.

Here's a recap of some of the things that have happened over the past ten months... With Mon and Zelle having possession of their money again, they took their portion of it and used the rest to pay off the people who were in their crew. They told them that they were stepping out of the game and that they didn't care what they did with their money. Some of them started hitting the streets on their own and a few partnered up to get some legit businesses started. No matter what they did, none of them worked for anyone else and none of them went emptied handed. The portion of the money that should've went to Chucky was given to his mother and siblings. If they did right by the money, they could invest it and be sitting on a pretty penny. But knowing his mother, she'd burn through that money within the next two years and be out here begging for more.

Like I said earlier, Mon and I learned that our son was indeed Mon's. Of course, with it being his first born, he was his father's namesake. He came out lookin' just like Mon. So much so people wondered what part I played in having him other than carrying him. That was okay because I knew that when he got older, he was going to be a splitting image of me. Although he was only five months, he was already spoiled. My father spoiled him more than anyone else, believe it or not.

India and Zelle were still together and happy as ever. India even went back to school and started working on the hours she needed to complete in order to graduate on time. It was hard as hell trying to balance everything out, but Zelle helped and it made things so much better for her. With as much as she did, I always made it a point to let her know that she was my 'Shero'. She hated when I'd praise her, but I always felt that a little complimenting could go a long way.

"We're here," Mon told me, removing me from my thoughts. We got out the car and went our separate ways. We'd be seeing each other soon. He gave me a hug and kiss and strolled away from me. I pranced towards my line, fixing my clothes as I went along.

"You ready, sis?" India asked, walking up to me and giving me a hug.

"I'm as ready as I'll ever be. What about you?"

"Girl, I was born ready. Let's do this," she told me, and we got in line.

Everything was like a blur. My mind was on everything but what we were there for. It wasn't until India hit me on the shoulder that I realized that it was our time to get up.

My nerves once again had gotten the best of me. It seemed like it was taking forever for me to make my appearance on the stage, but I didn't lose my cool. No matter how nervous I got, I still kept my poker face on.

India and I got in line. We slowly began walking to the front of the venue.

"Sianni Mitchell..." I took my time walking across the stage to receive my degree. Don't ask me how I did it, but I did. Mon paying Edward a visit worked out in my favor. He had no problems putting down that India and I had completed the required number of hours needed to get our Masters.

"Yaayyyyy... That's my baby," my mother yelled. I dropped my head a little because she'd embarrassed me. But when I got up to my professor, she pushed my head back up.

"Don't ever be ashamed of your parents loving you," she told me. That made sense because there were plenty of people who wish they had their mother and/or father around to continue to give them praise. With me having it, there was no reason for me to ever be ashamed.

"India Pace...."

"Come through, baby girl," Celia yelled out.

"I'm going right on through. Watch me walk, mommas," India yelled back. She started dancing across the stage. I laughed at her because she was a straight fool, but I didn't blame her one bit because after everything that we'd gone through, we still came out on top.

A few more names were called before they moved on to the next discipline. India and I stood on side of the stage patiently waiting.

"R'Mondo Willis..." As soon as my baby's name was called, I screamed as loud as I could. India was right along with me as well as our families and the crew. With everything that had happened with Mon and him not really having family there to support him, we wanted him to realize that even though we weren't his biological family, we were still his family.

When the ceremony was over, we all took a few pictures together before we had to turn our caps and gowns back in. Then we took the party back to our house. Mon and Zelle refused to let us come back home until we each had a new house built. Our homes were right next to each other, well, on the same land and there was a big black gate going around both homes. Nobody could get in unless they had a code or they were let in. That was to ensure we were safe. Even though Mon and Zelle walked away from the street life, we weren't crazy enough to assume they didn't have enemies out there somewhere. But we could guarantee that whenever those enemies decided to show their face, we'd be well protected.

When you met me, my life was in shambles. I was depending on my inheritance because I knew my parents were going to cut me off the minute I decided to live in the same household as Yosef. They said he wasn't the man for me and they were right. Now, my life was better than I ever expected it to be. Who ever would've thought I'd end up this happy by Creepin' with the Plug Next Door.

(The End...)

CPSIA information can be obtained
at www.ICGtesting.com
Printed in the USA
LVHW011650070820
662641LV00002B/198